THE MEG MILANO MASTER PLAN

Meg laughed but only a little. Now she wasn't quite so sure she wanted to leave her friends and go be a big star in the Gifted and Special Program with all the other smart kids in Camden. She and Molly had so much fun imagining themselves beating the Know-It-Alls at everything from spelling to word problems. But Molly hadn't gotten into the Gifted Program.

So far nothing was going according to the Meg Milano Master Plan.

Friends 4-Ever

P.S. We'll Miss You
Yours 'Til the Meatball Bounces
2 Sweet 2 B 4-Gotten
Remember Me, When This You See
Sealed with a Hug
Friends 'Til the Ocean Waves

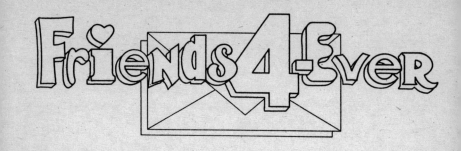

FRIENDS 4-EVER MINUS ONE

Deirdre Corey

AN
APPLE
PAPERBACK

SCHOLASTIC INC.
New York Toronto London Auckland Sydney

ISBN 0-590-44029-2

12 11 10 9 8 7 6 5 4 3 2 1   1 2 3 4 5 6/9

Printed in the U.S.A.   40

First Scholastic printing, March 1991

TO BEE OR NOT TO BE

Looking up at the stage from the third row, Meg Milano could hardly sit still. Her fingers were tapping madly on the armrests, as maps of the world flashed through her mind like a slide show. All around her, the auditorium was abuzz with the voices of kids practicing the names of state capitals, South American rivers, and African deserts for the Camden Schools geography bee, and Meg was just one more round away from being up on that stage herself.

"Your foot's tapping on the back of my seat again," an older woman said when she turned around to scold Meg.

"Sorry," Meg apologized. "Be still, foot," she whispered to her right foot.

"Here," said Stevie Ames, holding out a stick of cinnamon gum. "Chew on this while you're waiting. That's what I do if I get nervous before a big soccer game."

"I'm not nervous," Meg explained, "just excited. And when I'm excited my feet don't know they're attached to the rest of me."

Even the woman in front laughed a little, along with half of row C where Meg was seated with her parents and best friends. Stevie Ames, Laura Ryder, and Laura's pal Shana McCardle had all come to cheer on Meg as well as Molly Quindlen who was in the finals, too.

After a month of quizzing each other on geography facts, Meg and Molly were walking atlases who knew that the source of the Nile River was in East Africa and that the capital of New York State was Albany, not New York City. Nothing was going to stop Molly and Meg, two of the Friends 4-Ever. They could already picture themselves touring the White House on the Washington, D.C., trip they knew they were going to win. There was just one last hurdle.

"I can't believe you might wind up against the Know-It-Alls if they win this round," Laura Ryder whispered down the row to Meg. "Especially since Molly and I already had to audition against Erica and Suzi for the ballet recital."

Even more than Meg, Molly was determined to win the bee. She hadn't looked up from her clipboard of geography facts for days, except to eat and sleep. The fact that she and Laura had recently gotten bigger ballet parts than Erica and Suzi, the two most obnoxious girls in school, well, that was ancient history. Today's subject was geography.

"Our next two competitors come from Crispin Landing Elementary," a voice boomed out over the hum of voices. "Please welcome Erica Soames and Suzanne Taylor."

"The Know-It-Alls," Stevie cackled as she clapped just her pinkie fingers together.

Meg studied her two rivals. Erica and Suzi made their way to the stage as if they were about to collect a million dollars, instead of just having to guess the locations of places like Zambia and Tunisia.

"They must think it's a Halloween bee with those getups," Stevie muttered at the sight of the two girls. Both Erica and Suzi were dressed in the teeniest of black miniskirts, dark-colored tights, and oversized tops. Stevie just couldn't understand why anyone would go squeeze themselves into something as uncomfortable-

3

looking as a miniskirt. What if they suddenly wanted to shoot a few baskets, take a quick bike ride, or play in a pickup soccer game? Stevie was on sports alert at all times, and that meant comfortable faded jeans and high-top sneakers, not minis.

"You look great in that suspender skirt," Laura said when she noticed Meg staring enviously at Erica's and Suzi's outfits. "Red's your color."

"Thanks, Laura, but now I wish I hadn't begged my mom for this dumb skirt," she whispered so her parents wouldn't hear her at the end of the row. "It's so babyish, and so are these stupid socks." She pointed to the double pairs of baggy red and white socks that had looked so cute in the mirror at home.

"Now stop it." Laura reached across Stevie's lap to pat Meg's knee. "You look great, not like you're going to a funeral."

"Well, if they ask anything about Kansas or the Midwest when I get up there," Molly said, finally taking a break from her clipboard, "the Know-It-Alls will wish they *were* going to a funeral!"

"Enough with the clothes already," Stevie interrupted. "Check out that thing they always do

4

with their hair. They're going to get whiplash if they don't watch out."

Sure enough, when Meg looked up, Erica and Suzi were tossing back the long straight bangs that fell over their eyes just so. They were the only girls in Meg's grade with really short hair, which they went all the way to Providence to have cut. As they never stopped reminding everyone, none of the haircutters in Camden knew the right way to keep the back short and the front long the way they wanted. Whenever Meg had a chance to stare at them without being noticed, she studied these Providence haircuts and tried to imagine herself looking like that.

"Just for once, I wish I had straight hair," Meg groaned, trying to flatten her "boingies," the blonde curls that seemed to bounce around even when the rest of her wasn't moving.

"Just for once? Just for once?" Stevie sputtered, tangling her fingers in her own reddish-blonde strands going every which way. "You say that every day! Let's face it, Meg, we have hair that won't obey. But at least we don't go around dislocating our collarbones like those two!"

"They look like trained penguins when they do that head toss thing," Laura observed, stroking her thick dark hair, which was long and was going to stay that way forever.

Hearing that coming from quiet Laura, the girls hooted with laughter. When Meg stopped laughing, she felt happy and confident again. So what if the Know-It-Alls dressed like eighth-graders? They didn't belong to the Friends 4-Ever, did they? They didn't have their best friends coaching them at club meetings and cheering them on like her friends, did they?

No, they did not.

Friends 4-Ever had been Meg's great idea for a pen pal club to stay in touch with Molly during the long, horrible time she had lived in Kansas. Now that Molly was finally back, they didn't really need a pen pal club anymore, but they would always need each other. So the four girls still got together for meetings and wrote each other little notes on their special stationery to share their feelings and problems. The latest problem was for one of them to beat the Know-It-Alls in the geography bee and win that trip to Washington.

"Now from Roaring Brook School, please welcome Rebecca Bishop."

"Poor her," Meg murmured to Molly as a terrified-looking girl climbed the stage steps.

The geography bee official tapped on the microphone, and the sound of static made Meg jump in her seat. The man turned to the girl from Roaring Brook School. "Now for your first question. Please name three of the six Balkan countries."

"They mostly end in *a*. I know that, I know that," Meg whispered to Molly. "Let's see. Mmm. Yugoslavia's one."

As the girl stood frozen onstage, Molly mouthed the words, "Albania, Bulgaria, Romania."

"Bacteria, hysteria, cafeteria," Stevie muttered down the row to Laura and Shana who had also lost during earlier rounds back at Crispin Landing Elementary School a few weeks before.

A loud buzzer went off, putting a stop to all the whispering and jokes in row C. "I'm sorry, but your time is up. The answers are — "

" — Albania and Bulgaria," Suzi Taylor broke in, leaning toward the microphone even though it wasn't her turn.

"And parts of Greece, Romania, Turkey, and Yugoslavia," Erica Soames added smugly although it wasn't her turn, either.

"What show-offs!" Meg said during the applause. "I could have answered that, too, but I wouldn't hog the microphone and embarrass that Roaring Brook girl." Meg could already picture herself being the kind of winner who would shake hands with the losers and not give answers when it wasn't her turn.

"Please give a hand to all our contestants," the official said when the round was over. "There will be a fifteen-minute break for our winners Erica Soames and Suzanne Taylor. Then we'll start the next round."

"Ooo," Meg squealed. "We're next. I'm going to go stretch my legs. Coming, Molly?"

"No, I want to study some more," Molly said. "I'm going to sit here while it's quiet."

As Meg turned away she could hear Molly mumbling things like "Yangtze River" and "Walla Walla, Washington."

"Well, you look ready to take on the geography whizzes," Mr. Milano said when Meg ran over to her parents who were talking with the Quindlens in the aisle.

"I am, I am," Meg said breathlessly. "I knew practically all the answers way before the kids onstage."

"That's great. Now all you have to do is take things slowly," Mrs. Milano advised. "Use the whole minute to think of your answers if you need to."

"I know that, Mom," Meg groaned, "but I didn't need a whole minute while I was practic-

ing. I got the answers even before the Know —
um, Erica and Suzi did. Really."

Mrs. Milano looked doubtful. Oh, how Meg
hated that look! She knew it would soon be followed by more advice and practical tips that Meg
wouldn't want to hear. Mrs. Milano had been a
teacher before she started writing newsletters for
doctors and dentists. She was always giving Meg
suggestions about schoolwork. *And* about floss-
ing! "You know, if you feel nervous, just take a
few deep — " Mrs. Milano went on.

"I'm fine, Mom. I know this stuff inside out,
and I'm going to do great. So just start packing
for Washington, okay?" Meg asked before she
turned away so her parents would start talking
to the Quindlens instead of driving her crazy.

"My mother keeps forgetting she's my mom
and not a teacher anymore," Meg complained
to Laura.

"Yeah, but look how far you got, Meg. All
that coaching paid off. I wish I were still in the
bee with you and Molly," Laura sighed. "If only
they'd asked questions about *Anne of Green
Gables*."

"Prince Edward Island, Canada," Meg piped
up, naming the location of Laura's favorite book.

"Ugh, would you cut it out already?" Stevie
groaned. "You and Molly are like walking

globes. I can't wait 'til this is over, and we can go back to talking about whatever we used to talk about before you and Molly turned into encyclopedias. Look at her over there mumbling away. It's absotively posolutely abnormal."

Meg had to agree. "Laura, see if you and Stevie can unglue Molly from her clipboard," Meg suggested. "Maybe she'll listen to you. She's cramming again. You know how she gets."

"And we know how *you* get, Meg Milano," Stevie broke in. "Carried away. Overconfident. Like what happened with *The Magic Princess* when you got stage fright and your voice got shaky. When my brother, Dave, coaches me he says a little fear is a good thing."

"Well, this isn't a soccer game, so what's there to be afraid of?" Meg protested. "I know all my continents. I can picture their rivers and mountains and crops — everything. I even remember the color of each country on the globe."

Stevie sighed. "Well, we all know your mind's a computer, Meg, and that you even file your socks. But don't get carried away. That's all I'm saying, okay?"

"Okay, okay," Meg answered impatiently. "But Molly's the one who's a wreck. How can we get her to relax, anyway?"

"We can't," Laura broke in. "Ever since she

got back from Kansas, she's been trying out for everything in sight. You name it."

"Ballet, horseback riding, this crazy geography bee," Stevie recited. "I hardly ever see her. And she's been a grump ever since she found out she didn't get into G.A.S.P."

"Stevie!" Laura shushed. "Don't even mention the Gifted and Special Program with Molly around. You know how upset she is that Meg got in and she didn't."

"Sorreee," Stevie apologized. "I can't believe anybody'd be upset about not getting into something where you get double schoolwork."

"It's an honor," Meg said proudly. "Like you getting on the Select soccer team. I just wish Molly had gotten in, too. I try not to talk about it around her, but it's going to be hard once I start."

"I think that's why Molly's so determined about this geography bee," Laura said, sounding concerned. "It's like she has to win everything ever since she came back. She's afraid everybody'll think she's behind because she was in Kansas so long."

"Well, let's give her a fake report card or something so she stops moping about that stupid program," Stevie said.

Shana giggled, and her little parrot earrings

11

swayed back and forth from her ears. "It's not a stupid program, Stevie, it's for the smart kids. Not like us."

"Don't say that, Shana," Meg protested. "Look how great you're doing since I've been tutoring you."

"Well, I'll never be a brain even if Albert Einstein tutored me." Shana paused. "Is that his name?"

Meg laughed. "Yeah, but he's dead, so he couldn't tutor you."

Both girls laughed, then watched to see whether Stevie and Laura could coax Molly out of her seat on the other side of the auditorium. "You need to move, stretch out," Laura was saying to Molly when the girls rejoined them. "Do what we do in ballet for warmup. C'mon now, tighten your leg muscles. Now relax them."

Molly rolled her eyes. "This isn't ballet. There's nothing wrong with my legs, it's my brain. I need to keep studying, not stretching my leg muscles." All the same, with the girls looking on, Molly reluctantly shook her arms, then stretched each of her cowgirl-booted legs.

"Uh-oh," Shana interrupted. "That guy in the weird plaid jacket just came back onstage. You guys are about to go on, ready or not."

"Good luck, Meg." Mr. Milano patted Meg's head before she ducked.

"Don't forget, take your time," Mrs. Milano advised. "And — "

" — and nothing, Mom. I'm ready. Ask me anything. Washington, D.C., here we come!" Meg said just as she heard her own name announced.

"That's us!" Molly cried.

Suddenly Meg was the one nailed to the floor. She could hardly hear the applause over the *kerthunk kerthunk* of her heart. She didn't have time to flatten her hair, smooth her skirt, check her socks, or do anything she had planned before getting up in front of the whole town. Somehow — she didn't know how — she got to the stage, and her family and friends became part of a sea of dots in the audience.

When her eyes and ears finally came into focus and her heart *kerthunk*ed a little more slowly, Meg zeroed in on Erica and Suzi. There they were, standing onstage as if they did this every day. Was it possible that they were a whole head taller than Meg and Molly? Did wearing black make you grow mysteriously? In her little red skirt, Meg felt like a kindergartner competing against high school students.

"Our first question is for Molly Quindlen.

Please name the Kansas state anthem."

Goody, a Kansas question, Meg thought. One for the Friends 4-Ever side. But Molly didn't look as confident as Meg felt about the question, and it was awfully quiet up on the stage and in the audience as everyone waited for Molly's answer.

Think, think! Meg urged Molly on silently when the seconds ticked off one by one and Molly didn't answer. "Home on the Range," Meg repeated in her head. Maybe she could somehow beam the right answer to Molly by mental telepathy.

"*BZZZZZZZ, BZZZZZZZ,*" rang the awful minute buzzer a split second before Molly cried out the right answer: " 'Home on the Range'! 'Home on the Range'!"

"I'm sorry. 'Home on the Range' is correct, but the buzzer went off before you answered."

Meg heard Molly sigh like a tire losing air. "Sorry, Molly," she breathed, but her friend just brushed by her as she left the stage. Across the way, Erica and Suzi could barely hide their mean little smiles and aimed them straight at Meg.

"Margaret Milano, here is your first question. In what country is the highest mountain in the western hemisphere located?"

Meg's mind was blank. She barely knew what state she was from, let alone what hemisphere.

14

She felt lightheaded, almost dizzy as the ugly black hands of the huge minute timer on the stage reminded her that the remaining seconds were disappearing fast. The hot overhead lights and the hum of the audience waiting for her answer brought back all her old terrible *Magic Princess* feelings — the sweaty palms, the rubber legs, and the awful feeling that if she tried to speak nothing would come out.

Squinting out into the audience, she caught a glimpse of Laura's encouraging smile and Stevie's thumbs-up sign. The sight of her friends unlocked her mind, and some tiny brain cells started talking to each other.

With two seconds left, she cried out, "Argentina?" just ahead of the buzzer.

"That is correct," the official said before turning to Erica and Suzi.

Meg tried to relax while the Know-It-Alls rattled off their own answers like United Nations guides. But all too soon the official was back to Meg with another tough question.

"Please name the capital of Nigeria," the man said to Meg.

Lagos? Monrovia? Which one was it? Meg frantically asked her brain as the clock ticked away. Forgetting everything her mother told her about taking the full amount of time to think through her answer, she blurted out, "Monrovia."

"I'm sorry. Monrovia is the capital of Liberia. You were close, but Lagos is the capital of *Nigeria*," the official told Meg. "A natural mistake. Thank you for participating."

"An unnatural mistake," she groaned to her friends when she went back to her seat in the audience. "You were right, Stevie. I was overconfident. I should have slowed down." Meg didn't dare look at her mother. Hadn't she told Meg to take things slowly, to stop and think? Ugh, it was too horrible.

"Never mind," Laura said. "I just wish the Know-It-Alls would leave for Washington right this minute."

"With a one-way ticket," Stevie added.

The girls straggled out of the auditorium not looking anything like the bouncy, happy group that had gone in. What didn't help was seeing a crowd of middle school kids who were gathered around Erica and Suzi. Meg couldn't hear exactly what they were all talking and laughing about, but she could have bet she heard her own name and Molly's, followed by gales of laughter.

"You'd think they won the World Series or something," Meg grumbled when the huge group surrounding Erica and Suzi swarmed by

16

in the parking lot. "I sure wish we had another crack at them."

"And I wish the ballet recital weren't so far away," Laura said to make everyone feel better. "We'll be the ones out front then, right, Molly?"

"Sooner than that," Molly said mysteriously. "Sooner than that."

"Too bad they don't give trips to Washington for being a good tutor," Shana told Meg. "You're way better than that Erica any day of the week. All she used to do was yell at me when I didn't know stuff."

"Well, knowing where the Fiji Islands are won't help them when soccer starts," Stevie said, already picturing how she would keep Suzi and Erica away from the ball. "I guess it's up to you, Meg. Better start brushing up on your decimals and history dates or whatever it is they teach in those G.A.S.P. classes." Stevie grabbed herself around her neck and sucked in big gulps of air.

Meg laughed but only a little. Now she wasn't quite so sure she wanted to leave her friends and go be a big star in the Gifted and Special Program with all the other smart kids in Camden. She and Molly had had so much fun imagining themselves beating the Know-It-Alls at everything from spelling to word problems, after winning the geography bee, of course. But Molly hadn't gotten into the Gifted Program, and it turned out that Meg didn't know the difference between Liberia and Nigeria.

So far nothing was going according to the Meg Milano Master Plan.

THE MESS

Meg was afraid to pull off the plastic sheet lying over the workbench. Unless some elves had come along in the last few weeks to finish her science project, she was pretty sure there was going to be a mess of sand and clay underneath. While she had been memorizing capitals, rivers, and lakes, her science project had been lying unfinished on the workbench in the cellar.

"Yeow, yeow." Meg heard a whiny complaint and felt a furry meat loaf brush against her ankles.

"You already had dinner, silly cat," Meg said to Marmalade. "Sometimes we come down here for other reasons, you know."

Marmalade didn't know anything of the kind. His bowl was in the cellar, so why would anyone go down there unless it was to feed him? As

19

Meg made her way to the workbench, Marmalade lay on his orange back to show off his large snowy-white stomach. This amazing trick usually brought on the cat food, but this time it didn't work.

Meg ignored the white belly, the whiny begging, and the ankle rubbing. Instead, she peeled away the black plastic, and there it was. The Mess. What was going to be a wonderful geology model of the town of Camden was just a wooden board with lumps of grayish plaster and piles of sand and rocks scattered about.

Meg groaned. This wasn't quite the project that was going to help her get over losing the geography bee to the Know-It-Alls, that was for sure. Even Marmalade didn't want to be anywhere near The Mess and bolted upstairs.

Meg shivered. She didn't much like being in the damp basement by herself and hoped her friends would get there soon. They had all spent so much time coaching each other on geography that they were miles behind on their science projects. Tonight they were going to try to catch up.

"Need some more light, Mego?" Mr. Milano called from the top of the stairs.

"No thanks, Dad." Meg sure hoped her dad wasn't going to come down and "help" out. The last time that happened Meg's collection of rocks from different places around Camden had turned into — The Mess. Her dad had started talking about all the great science projects he'd done when he was a boy, and the next thing Meg knew, they were driving around town taking pictures of rock faces and outcroppings and planning the whole thing out on graph paper. Mr. Milano had made it sound so wonderful, Meg thought it would be fun, like making the dollhouse furniture and the cozy hotel houses they'd built together a couple years before.

"How's it coming?" Mr. Milano bent over the workbench and moved two or three rocks into different positions. "Did that plaster of paris dry okay?"

Why didn't he go away? Meg didn't want to hurt her dad's feelings, but it was supposed to be her project, wasn't it? "I'm not finished with those yet, Dad." She moved the rocks back to where they had been.

"Sure, sure, Mego. This is the neat part of science, isn't it? Trying this, trying that?" Mr. Milano clasped his hands behind his back to keep from touching the rocks again.

"I know, Dad, that's what I was going to do." Meg squeezed herself between her dad and the workbench.

"Well, if you need me, just whistle," Mr. Milano said, but he didn't leave quite as fast as Meg hoped.

She did want to do a good job. She wanted to do a *great* job, a super job, a Meg Milano kind of a job. Science was practically her best subject, and Mr. Retzloff was the best science teacher in the whole world. No one had ever submitted a geology model of their town before, he'd told her, and she was just the one to do it. Meg remembered Mr. Retz's words of praise, and in no time she'd been carried away.

As usual.

If only her parents would stop "helping out," then maybe she could get the project finished before it turned into a life-sized version of their town instead of a simple geology model! The sound of more footsteps on the cellar stairs saved her from any more thoughts about being buried alive under granite boulders and pyrite rocks.

Mrs. Milano came over to the workbench to admire Meg's project. "This is going to look great. You know, if you add a little red food coloring to the plaster of paris, it might look like the sandstone hill on Warburton Avenue."

"Not tonight, Mom," Meg sighed. "I just want to lay everything out. I don't want to get into the messy stuff until I know where it's all going."

"You're right," Mrs. Milano agreed. "Hey, don't forget. With that new computer program I got for my newsletters, I can make some nifty labels. They'll look so professional."

"I already made the labels, Mom, remember?" Meg reminded her mother. "The stick-on kind with my own handwriting. Mr. Retz says that's okay."

"Well, I just thought, you know, it's so easy on my computer. I could just run off the labels while I'm doing my other work, that's all," Mrs. Milano said hopefully.

"They're already done, Mom, but some of this other stuff isn't, and I want to get more finished before Stevie, Laura, and Molly get here, okay? I have to help Shana out, too, so I can't really talk now."

"Okay, just wanted to let you know I'm here if you need me," Mrs. Milano said.

I need you to go, Mom, Meg thought, but she didn't say it out loud. Meg didn't often wish for brothers and sisters, but tonight it would have been handy having another kid around to distract her parents.

Braaang, braaang! Meg heard next just as she was reorganizing her rocks.

"Stevie! Can you try not to scare me to death?" Meg cried after she'd whirled around to see what was making such a terrible noise. "What is that thing, anyway?"

"My burglar alarm. It finally works." Stevie was holding up a tangle of wires, batteries, and part of what looked like a bike bell. "Now all I have to do is figure out how to hook it up to my backpack, and I'm done."

"I can't believe the Burglar Bag is scientific."

"Mr. Retz said it was okay. I mean, I could have done a model of the state of Rhode Island like you, I guess," she said with a nod toward Meg's project, "but our cellar isn't that big."

Laura, too, arrived with a small box of items she needed for her project on water pollution. "How's yours coming along?" Meg asked, only too glad to forget her huge project for a few minutes.

"You won't believe this, but the seeds I watered with the water from the stream out in back of my house haven't even sprouted yet. The ones I watered with water from upstream are already little plants."

"I wish I'd stuck with my Camden rock garden idea," Meg said when she looked at the neat row of bottles Laura had lined up. Laura's project looked so orderly, so complete.

"Somehow I can't see you with just an egg

carton of rocks, Meg," Stevie said, tossing a chunk of pyrite in the air and catching it behind her back. "I mean, it wouldn't look great. You being such a scientific genius, you can't do something simple like my Burglar Bag."

Braang! Braang! the awful alarm rang again.

"Cut it out, Stevie. We're supposed to be meeting to get work done, not fooling around," Meg told Stevie.

"Excuuuuse me! I forgot. We're serious scientists. No fun allowed." Stevie grapped a pair of safety glasses from above the workbench and did her best to look like a serious scientist, all frowns.

While Laura wrote out labels for her water bottles and Stevie worked unsuccessfully at connecting her burglar alarm to her backpack, Meg tried to remember just what it was she was supposed to be doing on her own project. She had started it so long ago. "Where's Molly, anyway?" she asked to distract herself. "We were all supposed to be here by seven."

At that, Laura reached into her jeans pocket and pulled out a crumpled piece of paper. "I forgot. Molly left this note in my birdhouse. Here read it. Maybe you can figure it out."

Meg smoothed out a sheet of Molly's rainbow stationery and began to read:

I'll be at the meeting,
but I'm going to be late.
I have something new, but
You'll have to wait.

                      Friends 'til your head stands,

Molly

"I wonder what she's talking about." Meg looked puzzled and a little annoyed. She liked everyone to be on time for any Friends 4-Ever meetings. People were supposed to follow the plans, and tonight's plans were to get the neglected science projects into prizewinning shape. Meg could hardly help her friends do that if they were going to clown around or show up late.

Of course, Molly *had* written a note, Meg reminded herself. The girls used their Friends 4-Ever stationery all the time to send each other messages, and each girl even had a special hiding place to receive them. Stevie's was in her favorite climbing tree, and Laura's was in the birdhouse in her front yard. Meg got all her notes in a fence knothole, and Molly's secret messages appeared in the knotted string of her old hammock.

"Maybe Molly's even more behind than we are, and she's too embarrassed to come to the meeting," Stevie suggested. "You know Molly. She's got her mind set on getting a blue ribbon at the science fair."

Meg put her hands on her hips and turned to Stevie in a huff. "Well, what's wrong with that? I want to win one, too. Don't you?"

"With the Burglar Bag? I'll be lucky if I come in last," Stevie answered. "What I really want to do is make sure that Evan Koslow — and my brothers — don't keep snitching cinnamon gum from my backpack. That'll be better than any ribbon."

Meg measured out some sand into a cup. "How about you, Laura? You want to get a ribbon, don't you? Then we'd really show those Know-It-Alls."

Laura's dark eyebrows were knit in concentration. "All I care about is finding out what's making this water so yucky," she said, holding up a glass jar of cloudy water. Everything about Laura was shiny and clean. Her hair was always smooth, her socks never fell down, and her jeans always looked as if they came straight from the dryer. She looked neat all the time and definitely did not like the very un-neat look of her water samples.

"Speaking of yucky, here I am with my project," a voice said from the stairs. Shana Mc-Cardle bounced down the steps, barely hanging on to the plastic box she had under one arm.

Meg rushed over to take Shana's things before anything inside spilled. With Mr. Retzloff's permission — and Meg's help — Shana had invented her own makeup for her science project. Meg peered into the box to see how far Shana had come along.

"I need major help," Shana confessed, in between snaps of gum. "The lip glop I made dried up since I worked on it a couple weeks ago. And look at this." She pointed to her streaky eyelids.

"What is that green stuff, anyway, and why's it all stripey?" Stevie wanted to know.

"It's supposed to be blue eye shadow I made with watercolors. I mixed it with baby powder, but it streaks and turns green when it touches skin."

"Frankenstein makeup! Sell it for Halloween," Stevie suggested. "Scare all your friends."

"Stevie!" Meg scolded. "We have to help Shana fix her hypothesis, or Mr. Retzloff won't give her a good grade. C'mon, Shana, let's figure out what went wrong here."

"Hypothesis, schmipothesis," Stevie said, doing her best to make Shana laugh. Shana did make a funny face at Stevie but obediently followed Meg to the workbench where they could get a better look at her makeup experiment.

Shana McCardle had started out as Laura's friend the year before when both girls were in the After-School Program on the days their mothers were at work. But now she was everybody's friend. This year, she and Stevie were in the LEAP program — Leapin' Lizards as they called it — so they could catch up on their reading skills. Molly liked the way Shana always traveled around with a bottle of nail polish and shared her teen magazines. And, of course, Laura still liked having Shana as a pal in what they'd nicknamed the "After-School Prison."

But the big surprise was that Shana and Meg had become friends, too. Meg had been jealous of Laura's new friend the year before and couldn't believe that quiet, sweet Laura was so chummy with someone who wore tight pants *and* had spiky hair. All that changed when Meg started to tutor Shana during study period. Now, of course, Meg Milano was determined to turn Shana into Meg Milano, Junior. Along with

29

study tips and math shortcuts, Meg was constantly giving Shana beauty advice about letting her spikes grow out or wearing plain sneakers instead of Day-Glo ones. Though Shana was doing much better in school, she wasn't about to flatten her spikes or wear boring sneakers. But everyone had fun watching Meg try.

"Where's Molly?" Shana asked while Meg mixed various potions into the eye shadow powder.

"We don't know," Meg sighed. "If we don't get all our projects done soon, we're not going to get *any* ribbons. I don't think I can stand the Know-It-Alls getting even more prizes. Suzi Taylor's mom is an engineer, and I know she does Suzi's projects for her. Remember that suspension bridge last year?"

"Yeah, but everybody knew her mother did it," Shana said, dipping a finger into the blue powder and rubbing it lightly on her hand. "Hey, it's not turning green. How come?"

"You needed something a little oily to make the molecules stable," Meg explained. "Now, do you still have that recipe we worked out for the pink lip gloss? Maybe you could mix up some more and put it in something airtight?"

"Like my head," Shana kidded, but Meg was too busy pouring, mixing, and sampling to laugh. This was serious business. Only the sound of the squeaky cellar door pulled Meg away from all the projects spread out on the workbench needing her expert attention.

"Where were you, anyway, Molly? Out measuring the speed of light?" Stevie asked when a frazzled-looking Molly came downstairs.

Meg's blue eyes opened wider than usual at the sight of her friend's three bulging bags. "What's in those?" Meg couldn't imagine how Molly's simple paper on horse breeding had turned into something that required these giant bags.

"You'll see in a minute," Molly said breathlessly. She put down the bags and pushed back the hairband that had slipped down her fine, chin-length brown hair.

"I have a feeling you're not in Kansas anymore," Stevie singsonged.

"If you mean, am I still doing that project on different breeds of horses, you're right, Stevie. I changed my *whole* topic," Molly announced. Her brown eyes were bright with excitement. "They're going to be sorry they didn't pick me for the Gifted and Special Program when they see this!"

Molly went straight to the workbench and cleared a big space for herself. With a great deal

of huffing, puffing, and bag crinkling, she un-
loaded heavy blocks of clay, several jars of paint,
and a box of pipe cleaners. Finally, with great
care, she slid out a huge piece of wood covered
with molded clay.

When everything was unpacked, Molly turned
to her bug-eyed friends. "Guess what it's going
to be!"

"An alien planet?" Shana guessed.

"Some kind of weird skateboard?" Stevie
asked.

Meg didn't have to guess. She knew. Those
clay shapes and mounds were as familiar to her
as her own backyard. Molly was making a model
of their town, too. She'd stolen Meg's idea!

"It's a topographical model of Camden, showing how streams and stuff feed into the reservoir
on Lake Road," Molly explained. "Of course, it's
nowhere near done. But this dent over here is
Patriot's Park Pond. That little blue squiggle and
those pebbles are the stream in back of Laura's
near the old Crispin Estate."

Meg swallowed so hard, she was sure her
friends could hear her. "Isn't that a little like my
project?" she asked, her voice getting high-
pitched and whiny.

"What do you mean, Meg? You're doing geology, rocks and stuff," Molly said. "Mine's to-

tally different. It's going to have water and trees and meadows, not just rocks."

The way Molly said the word "rocks" made Meg feel as if her own project were made of Play-Doh. She couldn't believe what Molly was doing — ruining both their chances of winning a ribbon. They would look like what they used to call copycatters, which everybody knew was worse than being a Know-It-All! "Does Mr. Retzloff know?" Meg finally found the voice to ask.

"It was his idea. I saw him the day after the geography bee and told him that I knew all about different kinds of maps and could I do something on that instead? He's the one who said a topographical model of the town would be good. Mr. Retzloff told me . . ."

Mr. Retzloff this, Mr. Retzloff that. Meg could hardly stand the thought that her favorite teacher had given Molly permission to do a project so much like her own. Didn't he remember how special he'd told Meg *her* project was? And couldn't Molly see they were practically the same thing?

"What about your horse-breeding chart?" Meg said desperately. Maybe Molly would realize how much better her old topic was than this new complicated one that looked just like Meg's.

"Pff." Molly curled her lip as if that idea were

something only a first-grader would want to do. "That's not going to get a blue ribbon. Besides, Melissa Golab is doing a chart on dog breeding, so then there would be two projects sort of alike."

"And this isn't?" Meg practically screamed.

"Isn't what?" Molly shot back.

"Isn't just like my project?" Two bright dots of pink stood out on Meg's cheeks as if they had been painted on. Her sky-blue eyes looked stormy.

"You think everybody's trying to copy you, Meg Milano," Molly said. "Well, I don't need to copy anybody to think of a good project. You're the one that gave me the dopey idea about the horses so you could hog the good ideas to yourself and nobody else could win. You were the one who kept saying I shouldn't study so much for the geography bee. You're the one who helped me with my essay about getting into the Gifted Program and look what happened."

For once Meg didn't have anything to say. As long as she could remember, she had always cooked up the plans for the Friends 4-Ever way before they even called themselves that. Thanks to her they'd had loads of clubs over the years and loads of projects, too. Why, everything from log houses at Christmas to summer sleepovers in the Milanos' backyard tent were Meg's ideas. She was always ready with her clipboard full of fun plans and jobs for everyone, and now Molly was mad at her for that.

"It wasn't my fault you didn't get into G.A.S.P.," Meg protested. "It's because you came back to school in the middle of the year," Meg said, repeating what the Friends 4-Ever had told Molly over and over when she didn't get into the Gifted Program.

Now she looked around to see if Laura, Stevie, or Shana would back her up, but they were doing their best to ignore the fight that was about to explode. Each one had her nose buried in *her* project. In fact, Stevie's nose was actually *in* her Burglar Bag.

"It's true, Molly. Don't you believe me?"

"Sure I believe you," Molly answered, holding up a perfect little clay tree she had made. "Now does anybody here have any glue?" she asked, also ignoring the fight that Meg was itching to start. "This tree won't stay up."

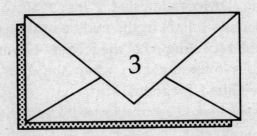

TEACHER'S PETS

Lots of kids crinkled their noses when they came into Mr. Retzloff's science room at Crispin Landing Elementary School, but Meg Milano wasn't one of them. She liked the weird smells in there, a mix of chemicals all jumbled up with the smell of the gerbils' cedar chips in the nature corner.

Today, the smell of the day in the science room was of something burning. "Now, don't try this at home, kids," Mr. Retzloff warned as he heated up an empty bottle.

Everyone in the room laughed the way they always did when "Mr. Retz" said this during one of his noisy, smoky, or fizzy experiments.

Even kids who hated science liked Mr. Retzloff, except for the Friends 4-Ever who actually *loved* him. Mr. Retzloff flung his Mickey Mouse tie over his shoulder so it wouldn't catch on fire while he demonstrated how to suck a whole egg down into a bottle.

"Ta dah!" he said, when the egg suddenly went down into the bottle. "Now, who can tell me why this happened?"

Immediately four hands shot up, and all of them belonged to the Know-It-Alls. Meg noticed that poor Rachel Garrity had to lean sideways so that Erica Soames' *two* madly waving arms wouldn't cut off her view.

"Come on, now," Mr. Retz coaxed, ignoring Suzi and Erica. "More than two people in this room must know the answer."

At least three people did, anyway, Meg thought, and she was one of them. She wanted to volunteer more than anything, but as usual when the big moment came, she couldn't do it. Every day she came to school determined to "participate" the way her teachers always suggested on her report cards. And every day when she got a chance, her heart started pounding, and she was afraid her voice would squeak instead of speak.

"C'mon, Meg, you know the answer," Laura

urged, though she was usually too chicken to raise her hand, either.

"I think their arms are going to fall off," Stevie muttered, with a nod to the hand-waving Know-It-Alls.

"Stevie, can *you* tell everyone why the egg went down into the bottle?" Mr. Retzloff asked when he noticed Stevie's lips moving.

"A new way to boil an egg?" Stevie joked.

"Close, Stevie, very close," Mr. Retzloff said with a straight face.

"Meg, how about you?"

Meg tried to keep the blood from rushing to her face, but she didn't have much luck. She was positive everyone in class was staring at her and just waiting for her to mess up. In fact, at that moment, Suzi Taylor sent a particularly evil look her way.

"When the warm air in the bottle cools, it creates suction that pulls down the egg," Meg mumbled.

"Good answer" — Mr. Retz beamed — "but could you say it a little louder?"

If only warm air under the floor would suck her down just like that egg, Meg thought desperately, then *she* could disappear from the class and not have to speak up again.

"WHEN THE WARM AIR IN THE BOTTLE

COOLS IT CREATES SUCTION THAT PULLS DOWN THE EGG," Meg repeated, sounding an awful lot like a robot voice in a video game.

"Great!" Mr. Retzloff said with a big smile before he went back to his desk.

"Teacher's pet," Erica muttered to Suzi Taylor.

"Meow, meow," Stevie purred. "They're jealous 'cause Mr. Retz always calls on you instead of them."

This was true, Meg realized. From the time Mr. Retzloff realized how good Meg was in science, he seemed to make a special effort to get her to talk in class. But he didn't always succeed.

For someone who liked nothing better than to go around running club meetings and directing her friends in crazy projects, Meg Milano had an unusual problem. She hated, just hated, talking in front of people she didn't know. It was that simple but very hard to change. Before any big event Meg was always positive she would get the biggest part, win the top prize, or answer the hardest questions. Then the big moment would come, and — *alakazaam* — super-confident Meg Milano would turn into a bowl of quivering Jell-O!

When Meg recovered from having to speak out loud, she heard Mr. Retzloff tell the class what to do next. "Now that you've all learned a new trick," Mr. Retzloff told everyone, "I want you to work on your science project outlines. You can sit with your buddy teams today."

"Yippee!" several kids shouted as the class regrouped into new clusters around the lab tables.

"Mr. Retzloff is soooo neat." Poor Laura was stuck in a different homeroom than her friends, and science was the only time besides recess and lunch when she could be with them. "Here, take this seat," Laura whispered to Stevie so that Molly would *have* to sit next to Meg.

Meg tried to concentrate on her science outline, but out of the corner of one eye she watched to see what Molly was going to do. Ever since the awful science project meeting, the two girls hadn't said even one word to each other. What Stevie and Laura found ridiculous was that both girls *pretended* they weren't even mad!

"Stevie, could you take this seat instead?" Molly asked when she came to the lab table.

"How come?" Stevie asked.

"I like that one better," Molly answered.

"Yeah, plus you're mad at Meg," Stevie taunted.

Molly's brown eyes narrowed. "I am *not* mad at Meg. I just want to sit *there*," she said, pointing to Stevie's stool.

"Well, I already warmed up this stool, so I'm not moving." Stevie gave Laura a secret look. They were going to force their two feuding friends to start talking no matter what.

The other tables around the room were filled with kids writing, talking, and helping each other. At the Friends 4-Ever table, though, one stool wasn't talking to the other stool. Meg pressed so hard on her pencil that the lead broke. As for Molly, she was practically *carving* out the words of her outline. At one point Meg and Molly accidentally touched elbows, and they pulled away from each other as if an electric shock had passed through them.

Meg was just rewriting her answer to the last question on the project outline when a shadow fell over her paper. "Looks like you're in good shape, Meg," Mr. Retzloff said when he read what she wrote. "Maybe when you're done you can work with Molly on her outline. We cooked up a new project for her, and she could use a friendly boost, right, Molly?"

Molly nodded so Mr. Retzloff would go away, but she didn't once look up or stop writing.

"Whoa, Molly, take it easy. You've still got plenty of time. Look at Stevie here, not a care in the world."

"That's 'cause I'm done, Mr. Retz," Stevie told

her teacher. "It's the Burglar Bag I'm having trouble with, not the outline about the Burglar Bag."

"Well, you know there's a space on my outline sheet where you have to describe your methods, so why don't you put a little more elbow grease into this part of the project, okay, Stevie?"

"All right," Stevie groaned before she climbed off her stool to get a pen from her backpack.

Down on the floor next to her backpack were Meg's and Molly's packs, neither one of them equipped with a burglar alarm.

"Can I borrow some paper and a pen from one of you?" she called up in Meg's and Molly's direction.

"Okay," they both said at the same time.

When Stevie resurfaced, she stuck Meg's kitten stationery under her outline sheet and slid Molly's rainbow paper under Laura's work. Turning away from Meg and Molly, she held up a piece of Meg's stationery, waved it at Laura, and made a lot of handwriting motions.

"Boy, you guys got busy all of a sudden. Don't worry, I won't copy," Meg observed a few minutes later when she noticed Laura and Stevie blocking their papers while they scribbled away. "What have you got there? Secret plans for a spy rocket or something?" Then she got so caught up in her own work, and in making sure she didn't touch Molly's elbow by mistake again, that she didn't see Laura and Stevie exchange their tenth secret glance of the morning.

With everyone trying to catch up on their outlines, the science room was fairly quiet now. Except for the Know-It-Alls. Erica and Suzi had finished their outlines early, so Mr. Retzloff gave them permission to talk quietly in the nature corner. They were just quiet enough so that Mr. Retz didn't have to tell them to lower their voices. But their whispers were loud enough to let the whole class know how *they* had finished early and how *they* couldn't wait to start in the Gifted and Special Program classes where the kids were sooo *advanced*. Ugh, Meg thought. This is what the G.A.S.P. classes were going to be like: the two Know-It-Alls versus one boingy-haired Friend 4-Ever.

When Meg bent down to get a sharper pencil, she sneaked a peek at Molly who was just reaching for her backpack, too. The contact between one pair of blue eyes and one pair of brown eyes was so unexpected, neither girl knew what to do.

"I have to talk to Mr. Retzloff," Molly said suddenly before she bolted from her stool.

"Aren't you going to help her, ever?" Laura

asked Meg after Molly left. "Stevie and I are going crazy watching you two. Now that Molly's doing a Camden project, anyway, why don't you both work together?"

Meg chewed on her pencil eraser. Laura was her best friend, but right then she wished she had a best friend who wasn't always so sweet and so nice and so darned understanding. Meg wanted to stew and pout and throw her pencil at Molly, and she just wished Laura wanted to do the same thing. But nooo, here was Laura trying to be the peacemaker all the time.

"Whose side are you on, anyway, Laura?" Meg blurted out, before a wave of shame nearly kept her from getting out the question.

"We're all friends," Laura answered softly. "We don't have sides. You two are just being so dumb, and now nothing's fun anymore."

"Yeah, it's like you two are in a contest with each other or something," Stevie said, trying to catch the drips coming from the lab sink faucet with her fingers. "This is worse than the geography bee, and I was hoping we'd get back to normal after that!"

"She copied my project," Meg repeated.

Laura opened and shut the rings of her binder over and over until she could think of what to say next. She snapped the rings twelve times straight before the answer finally came to her. "Did you ever think Molly might want to be like *you*, Meg? That *if* she copied your project, and I'm not saying she did, that maybe it's because she wants things to be like they used to be? Before she went to Kansas, you two were always the ones that were so smart."

"Even smarter than the Know-It-Alls," Stevie said, flicking drops of water toward the corner where Erica and Suzi were still whispering up a storm.

Meg's pencil eraser was all gummy now. There was nothing left to chew while she thought of a way to get her friends to look at her like she was Meg Milano, Super Friend, and not Meg Milano, Friendship Wrecker.

"Meg! Hey, Meg! Can you come over here for a second?" Mr. Retzloff called out.

"Go on, Meg. He's waiting," Laura urged. "They're waiting." She tugged Meg's hand, pulling her a few inches off the stool.

"Oh, all right," Meg grumbled. "Just as long as everybody knows I thought of *my* project first."

"We know, we know," Stevie groaned, giving Meg a push from behind. "And who cares, anyway? Sheesh!"

When Meg got to the desk, Mr. Retzloff was

busy with Molly's outline. "Mmm," he murmured while Molly and Meg studied each word of the fire safety tips on the wall so they didn't have to look at each other. "Mmm," he said again, making faint pencil marks on the paper. "You know, I think we've got something here, you two."

You two. Meg wanted to be part of the *you two* Mr. Retz was talking about. If only she and Molly hadn't gotten themselves into this — this *situation* — where somebody was going to have to say they were sorry or something embarrassing like that.

When Meg finished reading the fire safety chart, she stared at the floor. And when she stared at the floor, she saw two cowgirl boots. Inside those boots was the very friend she had missed for so long, the friend she had written so many letters to in Kansas. And now that they could say things to each other in person, they weren't even talking! Meg wished she'd never heard of the silly geography bee or the science fair or the Gifted Program or anything that forced her to compete with Molly.

"Take a look at this, Meg, and see what you think," Mr. Retzloff said with a smile when he handed her Molly's outline. "You two are my best experiment today."

When Meg began to read Molly's outline, she knew what her favorite teacher meant. Molly had written down all sorts of neat ideas about how the water and rock formations in Camden connected. Meg could see that Molly had found great stuff for Meg's project, and how Meg's information helped Molly's.

"I think you two should exhibit your projects together," Mr. Retzloff suggested.

"What do you mean?" Meg said, not quite ready to share her project with anyone else.

Mr. Retzloff leaned back on his chair, put his feet on the desk, and folded his hands across his chest, the way he always did when he wanted kids to really listen to his scientific explanations. Only this time Meg had a feeling his explanation wasn't going to be about science at all.

"Well, you know, Narragansett Electric is one of the science fair sponsors. And they kind of pay special attention to projects in earth science. Except for volcanoes, which everybody likes, you two are the only kids in my classes who really like the earth science part of science."

Mr. Retzloff looked at Meg. "See, you've got the geology stuff, and Molly, there, has the local watershed, and it all fits together. I was thinking if you both wrote up a little something extra about how it all ties in, the company might want to include your models in their earth science display at the library this summer."

Meg and Molly were speechless. Of course, Mr. Retzloff had no idea they had been speechless for nearly a week.

"Hey, I thought this would bring on the usual Niagara Falls of giggling," Mr. Retzloff said when he noticed his two students weren't falling all over themselves with shrieks at his good news. "I hope you two aren't still moping about that geography bee, now, are you? That's why I encouraged Molly to get herself a new topic so she could use some of what she knew about topographical maps."

"Is that really why?" Meg squeaked.

"That and the fact that I heard you girls were going to be separated when Meg here goes off to the Gifted Program three days a week. I thought having similar projects might keep my A Team together. So think about it, okay?" Mr. Retz said.

"Thanks," Meg mumbled. She didn't quite know what to do next. She was sure of one thing, though. She wasn't going to say anything that might make things worse.

When Meg and Molly got back to the lab table, Stevie and Laura seemed to be hard at work, so hard at work Meg should have been suspicious. But she was too busy trying to figure out what to do about Molly. First Molly slid onto her stool, so that's what Meg did, too. Then Molly opened her notebook, so Meg opened hers. When Molly picked up a piece of paper tucked into her notebook, Meg saw there was one in her notebook, too. Opening the rainbow-trimmed sheet, she began to read:

Dear Meg,
I know I look like a copycat
But believe me, I would never be that.
I admire your looks, I admire your brain.
I picked something new so we could be the same.
I don't know state anthems, forget about G.A.S.P.
But working together would be a blast!
                    Yours 'til the book ends,

                    Molly

Meg reread the piece of paper. It was Molly's stationery all right, but there was something not quite Molly-ish about this note.

When she glanced over at Molly, her friend was reading something, too, a note on Meg's kitten stationery! "Hey, what's that?" Meg wanted to know.

"Read it out loud, Molly," Stevie and Laura said at the same time. So Molly began:

Dear Molly,
I've got rocks in my project,
I've got rocks in my head.
To think you would steal from me
I was badly misled.
Let's hook up our brains,
And have fun from now on,
My bad, mad, sad feelings are practically gone!
Friends 'til the dew drops in,

Meg

"You guys did this, didn't you?" Molly asked Laura and Stevie, who were grinning as much as Molly and Meg now were.

"Us? Do you mean us?" Laura said in mock amazement.

"You two did write these, didn't you?" Meg asked.

"Yup," Stevie said. "We just wrote what you *would* have said if you both weren't so stubborn. Is that a crime?"

"A Friends 4-Ever kind of crime," Meg said. "The kind I like."

"Okay, now you have to both apologize," Laura told the girls. "For real. C'mon now. You go first, Meg. Start with 'I'm sorry, Molly.' "

"I'm sorry, Molly," Meg began. "I didn't *really* think you stole my idea. Well, at first I did think that, but now I think it's neat we can work on both our projects together."

"Very good, Meg. Your turn, Molly," Stevie said.

"I'm sorry I accused you of hogging everything," Molly said, looking serious at first. "It's just that it's taking me longer to get back into school again than I thought. Maybe we can go to G.A.S.P. together next year. Can I just be a little jealous, though?"

"Sure, and I'll be sad not to be in class with

you as much as we are now, but we'll be together all the time after school to work on our projects, the way Mr. Retz said."

Stevie handed Molly a lab beaker, and Laura handed one to Meg. "A toast, you two."

"To Molly," Meg said, clinking her beaker against Molly's.

"To Meg," Molly said, clinking back. "We'll miss you when you're in G.A.S.P."

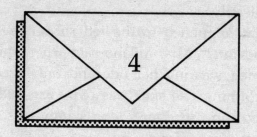

CAUTION: GENIUSES
AT WORK

"It's no use," Meg scolded the curly-headed girl in the mirror. She had dragged her meanest, pointiest hairbrush through her hair at least twenty times, but all that did was make her hair stick out even more. Finally, she got out the good old red-and-white polka-dotted hairband, the plastic one with the sharp teeth lining the inside, and pulled it across her scalp. There, now at least the top of her hair was lump-free.

While she was trying to slick down the rest of her hair with the palm of her hand, a second face appeared in the mirror.

"Excited?" Mrs. Milano asked, peeking around the door.

"Sort of," Meg said. She didn't mention the flippy sort of stomachache she was having or the cells in her body crying, "More sleep! We need more sleep!"

"What happened to the red suspender skirt you had out?" Mrs. Milano said when she noticed Meg wearing her one and only piece of black clothing. The skirt was two years old and a bit too short for Meg's long skinny legs.

"I felt like wearing this one, Mom," Meg answered.

Mrs. Milano bit her lip and looked as if she were about to say something else but didn't. "Breakfast'll be ready in two shakes," was all she said before going downstairs.

When Meg came into the kitchen a few minutes later, her dad gave her a huge smile. "Well, today's the day!" Meg loved the feeling those words gave her on birthdays, holidays, and going-on-vacation days — a feeling that something big was about to happen.

Something was. For the first time ever, Meg Milano was about to go to a new school without her best friends. As if that weren't enough, she was about to take her very first school bus.

"Sure you don't want a ride?" Meg's dad asked for the seventeenth time in the last couple of days.

"Just for this week?" her mother suggested for the hundred and seventeenth time. "Until you get settled?"

"No thanks," Meg answered for the millionth time. Half the reason for even going to the Gifted and Special Program was to take the bus to the middle school where the classes were held.

Mr. Milano was supposedly reading the paper the way he did every morning, but Meg could tell he wasn't paying any attention. For one thing, he was opened to the classified ads. "Backpack all set?" he asked.

"Mmmsh," was Meg's mushy, doughnuty answer.

"Got your watch?" Mrs. Milano asked.

Meg held up her arm to show that, no, she hadn't forgotten to wear the watch her parents had given her as a surprise when she got into the Gifted Program. Did they have some sort of checklist they were going through before she could leave the house? Socks? Check. Underwear? Check. Sneakers tied? Check.

"I guess the watch is in there somewhere, Meg, but it's a little hard to see under those diseased-looking string bracelets you have on," Mr. Milano said with a smile.

Meg looked down at her wrist. It was true. Her new watch was buried under a tangle of raggedy friendship bracelets she had been wearing for ages. Maybe Laura, Stevie, and Molly weren't going to the G.A.S.P. classes with her, but at least a little reminder of each one of them was tied to Meg's wrist.

"It's seven thirty-six and a half," she told her parents when she checked the watch. "I think I'll go now. Laura, Stevie, and Molly are meeting me in a few minutes. To wish me luck." Meg wrapped the rest of her doughnut in a paper napkin and handed the lump to her mother. "Can I have this when I get home, Mom? I'm not hungry right now."

"I wish you'd take one more bite." Mrs. Milano's voice trailed off. "Well, never mind. Just go have a super duper day, okay, sweetie? Here are some of those erasable pens you like and some extra erasers, too," she said, handing Meg a small plastic case of new supplies.

"Thanks, Mom." Meg just wished her parents weren't quite so excited. The both of them looked as though Meg were leaving for the University of Tasmania instead of the G.A.S.P. classes three days a week. And from the way her dad was beaming, Meg worried he was going to follow her right out the door and get on the bus, too! Before anything of the kind could happen, she raced to the front hall where she had put out her backpack the night before. " 'Bye," she yelled out, slamming the front door quickly just in case they were about to hand her a Snoopy lunchbox or a pair of galoshes!

Out in her yard, Meg automatically checked the knothole in the split-rail fence in front of her house. Like the post office mail, Friends 4-Ever letters came through rain, sleet, or snow. They even came on beautiful sunny Mondays, too, Meg realized when she wriggled her finger in the knothole and felt a piece of paper there. It was a note from Laura.

Dear Meg,

Would you believe my mom won't let me meet you at the bus stop? I mean it. She won't even let me deliver this letter, because tonight's Shampoo Night, and I might catch cold!!! Stevie's going to stick this note in your secret mailbox.

My mom says I'll be late for school or get a stomachache if I rush around in the morning. I hope my mom at least lets me wave at

the bus when you go by. (I can't wait to hear
what it's like to take the bus with all the older
kids!)

Good luck. I'll miss you. I hope you really
show those Know-It-Alls a thing or two or
three! I have After-School Prison today, so I
won't see you until regular school tomorrow.
Boo hoo!

Yours 'til the dew drops in,

Laura

Meg felt a tiny ache at the sight of Laura's familiar handwriting and her unicorn paper but no real-live Laura. She should have known the Ryders wouldn't let Laura run around so early on a school morning. Laura's parents were even more strict than Meg's, if that was possible. In fact, one of the reasons the girls were such good friends was because they both had things like Shampoo Night, Homework Time, Reading Time, Bedtime, and a whole schedule of things their families made them do at certain times. Poor Laura even had something she called Re-tainer Time when she was supposed to soak her retainer in some fizzy blue stuff and then scrub it. At least Meg didn't have *that* on her schedule!

"Boo!" Stevie shouted when she popped out

of the evergreens, next door to Meg's. "I see you got Laura's note. As usual, she's being held prisoner in her own house."

"Hi, Stevie. Yup, I got the note," Meg sighed. "I just knew her mother wouldn't let her out so early. They always go over her homework in the mornings, even after a weekend. Same at my house. Except for today, of course."

"You two should sue your parents," Stevie said. "I mean it. I saw this talk show, and these kids said their parents were too strict, so they — "

"I'm not going to sue my parents on the first day of my G.A.S.P. classes," Meg said, looking past Stevie to see if Molly was coming down the street. "I thought Molly would be here by now."

Stevie stopped chewing on the cold toast she had brought along. "Oh, she forgot to recopy her book report, so she said to tell you good luck. She didn't have time to write a note, but she'll call you tonight. So that just leaves me," Stevie said proudly. "And speaking of leaving, that's what I've gotta do, or I'll be late for school. Good luck. Break a leg or whatever. I don't know how I'm gonna get through school today without you reminding me about my books and homework and stuff."

"Thanks, Stevie. I'll miss you, too," Meg said,

but Stevie had vanished into the bushes that separated Doubletree Court from Half Moon Lane.

Down the road, Meg could see some older kids heading toward the footbridge that connected her Crispin Landing neighborhood to the next neighborhood over where the middle school and high school buses stopped.

"Hi, Meg," she heard a girl's voice say. "No school today?"

"Oh, hi, Amy," Meg said back. Meg had forgotten, totally forgotten, that Amy Gross was going to be on the bus, too. What if Amy suddenly announced, "Hey, everybody! I baby-sit for Meg Milano!" Thank goodness, Amy had no such plans and was much too busy talking to her own friends to embarrass Meg.

The hissing sound of the school bus brakes saved Meg from having to think about Amy anymore. When the yellow bus pulled up everyone surged on, and Meg did her best to squeeze in, too.

"C'mon, c'mon, I haven't got all day," a woman behind the wheel said to the last few stragglers. Meg turned around to see if the driver was talking to someone else, but no, she seemed to be talking to Meg. "You have a bus pass?"

Meg struggled to get at her brand-new pass,

which she had carefully put in the front pocket of her backpack.

"Never mind," the bus driver said. "Who'd get on this sardine can, anyway, if they didn't have to? You one of those gifted kids?"

Meg nodded and hoped no one had heard the driver's question. "You one of those gifted kids?" sounded almost like "You one of those two-headed frogs?" "You one of those purple-toed groundhogs?"

When the bus came to the next stop, everyone fell into each other as even more kids jammed onto the bus. Luckily this time, as the crowd moved backward, Meg spotted a seat and grabbed it.

The bus was moving up Church Street now, directly behind Laura's house. She could see Laura's back door and, lo and behold, she could see Laura waving at the packed bus! Laura's face was a blur, but a familiar friendly-looking blur. Meg wanted so badly to wave back, but she knew how dumb that would look. After all, no one would know she was waving to a real person!

As Meg settled back in her seat for the rest of the ride, she began to pick out individual voices from the jumble of conversation that filled the bus. Kids were talking about who to have lunch with, where to meet between classes, and how heavy their books were — the same kind of talk Meg always had with her own friends on the way to school. She missed Laura, Stevie, and Molly already, and she hadn't even gotten to school yet!

"I promised my brother I would do all his chores if he let me wear his varsity jacket today," Meg heard a familiar voice say.

"I just snitched Andrew's out of the front hall closet," a second familiar voice said. "We'll be the only ones in the middle school, I bet, with high school jackets. That'll be so neat."

Meg *knew* those voices. Finally, when the first girl spoke again, Meg solved the mystery.

"Mrs. Dunwoodie told my dad she can't wait to meet me," said Erica Soames in her loudest, braggiest voice. "When she saw him at the Board of Education meeting last week, she said she would look out for me. And you, too, of course, Suzi."

Meg's stomach did a backflip, and this time it wasn't because the bus was hitting every bump in Camden. Erica's father was on the Board of Education and had already told this Mrs. Dunwoodie about Erica and Suzi. So right away, the director of the Gifted Program would look out for the Know-It-Alls. Meg didn't know if she could stand it.

"Middle School! Everybody out for the Middle School," the bus driver yelled out a few minutes later.

Meg grabbed her backpack and pushed her way through the high school kids clogging the aisle. "S'cuse me. S'cuse me," she repeated, but just shoving her pack ahead seemed to work a lot better.

"Phew," a tall, skinny boy in a camouflage shirt said to Meg when the bus pulled away. "I think I left my right arm on the bus. Too late now."

Meg laughed. "Boy, am I ever glad I usually walk to school."

"Are you one of the gifted kids?" the boy asked Meg.

"Sort of," Meg mumbled, getting the two-headed-froggy feeling again.

"So where are the gifts?" The boy laughed as they walked into the building together. "What a dumb name, anyway. What's wrong with Brainbusters? Or the Smart Alecks? Or Teenage Mutant Geniuses? Speaking of names, mine's Chris Malone."

"I'm Meg Milano, and my friend, Stevie, nicknamed the Gifted Program G.A.S.P."

"Hey, pretty good," the boy said as he and Meg walked into the middle school together. "Anyway, I'll probably get kicked out for not being gifted enough. I'm already lost, plus I lost that letter they sent us telling us where we have to go."

Meg had her letter, of course, neatly tucked in with the unused bus pass. "It says here we should report to room 246. That'll be upstairs, I guess."

"Can't you just picture the gifted kids — big eyes and huge heads that kind of pulse in and out while they're thinking?"

"Ew, gross," Meg said.

By this time, several bells had rung, and the long wide halls had emptied out. Meg was glad she had someone to get lost with, even if it was a boy. The middle school looked so different from Crispin Landing Elementary School where she knew every scratch on the floor. In this school there were no finger-painted pictures, tissue paper daffodils, or cut-out alphabet letters lining the halls.

"Well, here it is, gasp, gasp," Chris joked. "Do you think everyone'll be wearing horn-rimmed glasses and carrying around calculators?"

"Hope not," Meg said.

In fact, there was one pair of horn-rimmed glasses in the room, and they were staring right at Meg and Chris when they came in.

"You must be Christopher Malone and Margaret Milano," the person behind the horn-rimmed glasses said crisply. "Here are your badges. I am Mrs. Dunwoodie, and I'm in charge of the Gifted and Special Program."

Meg took a stick-on badge and slid into one of the last empty seats around a huge wooden table. Erica and Suzi were already seated right by Mrs. Dunwoodie at the far end of the table and were acting like they were her assistants or something.

"I am pleased to welcome you to the Gifted and Special Program. I want to begin by saying that every person is gifted in some way no matter who they are. However, the Camden School System has decided to challenge those of you who have shown through tests and schoolwork that you have unusual gifts and abilities. . . ."

As Mrs. Dunwoodie droned on, Meg wondered what her own unusual gifts were. Always having a neat notebook? Perfect penmanship? An organized locker? What was she doing here, anyway?

". . . and I am honored to have the oppor-tunity to design and run this program so that all of you . . ."

. . . purple-toed groundhogs, Meg thought.

". . . can — with my help" — Mrs. Dun-woodie paused here to smile — "make the best use of your gifts and talents."

Whatever they are, Meg thought. When she looked up Chris was making snaillike antennae motions on his head as Mrs. Dunwoodie went into a new gear.

"Now for the nuts and bolts of what we'll be doing. Every morning, we will meet here from eight-twenty to eight-thirty. This can be a very creative and productive time," Mrs. Dunwoodie advised, "when you can think pleasant, peaceful thoughts, and open your mind for the new day ahead."

Meg couldn't help thinking about the ten free minutes back at Crispin Landing Elementary be-fore regular classes started. Usually she and her friends tried to squeeze in a day's worth of fran-tic conversation and plans before the first bell rang. Spitballs and flying erasers whizzed by, and if anyone was having peaceful thoughts about the day ahead, they didn't let on.

"Room 246 will be our home base, and many of our courses will meet here. I have fought hard to keep our program in this room where we can all sit around this table in a kind of seminar. Can anyone here tell me what a seminar is?"

Seminar? Did that mean they wouldn't be having their own desks? Meg wondered. She didn't have to wonder for long.

Mrs. Dunwoodie turned to Erica with a big smile. "Erica?"

Erica tossed back her head, and her bangs went with it. "Well," she began, "in colleges, the students sometimes meet with their professors in small groups to study and discuss a subject."

"I'll bet she has a dictionary opened to the *S*'s on her lap," Chris whispered to Meg who tried not to giggle.

"Very good!" Mrs. Dunwoodie exclaimed as if Erica had solved a complicated physics problem. "In all our *seminars*," she continued in the same syrupy voice, "we will be following the Socratic method. That means we will learn by asking and answering questions and sharing information in our group. I know everyone in the Gifted and Special Program will want to participate."

By the looks of things, the Know-It-Alls were ready to participate at any second. Every time Mrs. Dunwoodie asked a question, Erica and

Suzi and the same three or four other kids thrust their arms up in their hurry to answer first.

"I don't think I belong in G.A.S.P.," Meg complained to Chris when the group was dismissed to go to the science room. "I hate having to talk in class."

"Me, too," a familiar-looking girl said to Chris and Meg. "I'm Becky Bishop. I saw you at the geography bee. And you probably saw me freeze up in front of those two. 'Albania, Bulgaria, and parts of Greece,' " she said, tossing back her head and doing a pretty good Erica Soames imitation. "What a couple of show-offs!"

"Know-It-Alls," Meg corrected her, before she realized how mean that sounded.

Chris and Becky started laughing. "We've got kids like that from Roaring Brook, too," Becky said. "Certified geniuses."

"Not me," Meg sighed. "I don't even know the difference between Liberia and Nigeria. I can't figure out how I got picked for this, anyway."

"My parents made me come," Becky said. "They think if I'm in the Gifted Program that makes them gifted, too."

"Well, my parents didn't make me sign up, exactly," Meg answered, "but they sure bugged me about sending the forms back in a hurry. I didn't know we were going to be in these seminar things Mrs. Dunwoodie was talking about. You know, talking out loud all the time. My parents kept saying it would be lots of projects, stuff I like."

"Same here," Becky groaned. "Maybe if we get lucky everybody else will talk so much, we won't have to."

"I wish," Meg agreed. "Why did you sign up for the Gifted Program, Chris?"

"To get free gifts," he joked. "But seriously, folks, I heard they had something called Robots Alive and a class called Checkmate, which sounds way better than plain old math and stuff at Roaring Brook. Besides, my teacher wanted to get rid of me."

"C'mon," Meg said.

"He's right, Meg," Becky interrupted. "Chris is always getting checks next to his name on the board for drawing cartoons and turning the teacher handout sheets into weird space vehicles."

On cue, Chris pulled out a strange-looking spacecraft made out of the pink medical forms the kids were supposed to give Mrs. Dunwoodie. "See? Anyway, the school psychologist said I need to be challenged, so they sent me here with the mutant geniuses."

"Then I guess it's us against them," Meg said when they went into the science lab where the Know-It-Alls were already huddled with the teacher. With Meg leading the way, the three not-so-enthusiastic students headed for the seats as far back in the class as they could get without actually leaving the room.

It was going to be a long, hard day.

FALLING BEHIND

"You mean they actually call the newspaper *The Gifted Express*?" Stevie practically choked on her chicken wing. "You'd think they'd be embarrassed or something."

Meg waited for the information to sink in. Meg, Molly, and especially Stevie and Shana, were horrified and fascinated by Meg's tales of her first weeks in G.A.S.P. In fact, the best thing, practically the one and only good thing about G.A.S.P., was sitting in the cafeteria telling stories about it on the two days Meg was back at good old Crispin Landing Elementary.

"The Alpha group — it's sort of a buddy team only we can't stand each other — anyway, the

Alphas decided on the name. Not me and Chris, though. We thought we should name the newspaper *Kid Talk* or *Speak Out*, but nobody else liked our ideas. Finally Mrs. Dunwoodie told Suzi to decide since she's the editor. So, of course, it had to have 'gifted' in the title."

"Boy, am I ever glad I'm too dumb to get into a snobby group like that," Shana said.

"Me, too," Stevie agreed. "Plus I can hardly keep up with the stuff we have here. Especially without you around, Meg. I forgot to study for my *Wordly Wise* last week and thought *pygmy* had to do with pigs!"

Molly stopped chewing on her carrot stick and shook it at Stevie. "Stevie, I quizzed you a zillion times. I told you what *pygmy* meant, but you were too busy making pig jokes, remember?"

"Oink, oink, I know," Stevie said, making wet snuffling sounds. "It's just that when Meg tells me how to study she doesn't laugh at my jokes so we get more done. I know I'm going to fail school if you keep going to G.A.S.P., Meg."

Meg loved hearing how much her friends missed her and needed her. Though only two weeks had passed since the Gifted Program started, she felt months behind on all the fun she usually had with her friends. There hadn't been time for one single Friends 4-Ever meeting, not one. And she'd had to spend Friday night going with the G.A.S.P. kids to an *opera*, of all things, instead of the usual Friday night pizza at the Quindlens.

"I bet you're the smartest one there, huh, Meg?" Shana asked, smiling with pride at having such a brilliant friend.

If she only knew. In the last couple weeks Meg had learned things she had never known before, more than what *muons* and *trapezoids* were. Meg Milano had also discovered that kids her very own age not only won geography bees, but some of them wrote compositions that were published in real newspapers. One girl designed a poster that was shown all over the country telling people not to waste water. Another student invented a puppet character that got on a cable television show. It was hard to believe that a small town like Camden had so many geniuses running around.

"Well, we sure miss you, Meg," Laura said when she noticed the frown on Meg's face. "Of course, it's great without Erica and Suzi being such pains in Mr. Retzloff's."

"Mr. Retz! Omigosh! I forgot to study for his electricity test today," Meg cried. "I had to work on my *Gifted Express* article last night at the library, then I was supposed to study for the test when I got home. But I totally forgot."

"No, you were supposed to come over to my house, remember?" Molly said. "To help us plan the Easter egg hunt for the little kids in the neighborhood. Then we were going to work on our projects."

Meg slapped her forehead. "I think I need a bigger assignment book for all the new stuff I have to do. I had to fake my way through the math test last week and only got a B on it."

"Hey, give that B to us if you don't want it," Stevie said. "Shana and I got — "

Shana shook her head back and forth. Though her mousse-slicked spikes didn't move an inch, her hoopy earrings swayed back and forth. "Don't tell, Stevie. I'm too embarrassed."

Meg felt awful. On Monday night, the night before the math test, she had to cancel her tutoring time with Shana so she could work on her Future Cities project for G.A.S.P. "You didn't flunk, did you, Shana?" Meg asked now.

"Not exactly, but I don't think I'm going to get an engraved invitation to the Gifted Program after that test, either."

"I'm sorry. Maybe tomorrow night," Meg said. "Oh, no, I can't do it tomorrow night since that's the only time I have to work on my science project. I haven't done much on it since you guys came over." It seemed ages ago, Meg thought — before she became a mutant genius.

"Yeah, but don't worry," Shana said. "My mom can help me."

"Doesn't she work at Casa Miguel's on Thursday nights?" Molly asked.

"Yeah, but if the restaurant is slow, she runs to the apartment on her breaks," Shana said. "Or sometimes the owner lets me sit near the kitchen and do my work so my mom can help me between customers."

Now Meg realized she was missing something more important than Make-Your-Own-Sundae Day at Crispin Landing Elementary. She was missing her friends. She was letting them down, all because of being in G.A.S.P.

"Let's all go to the courtyard for the rest of the lunch period and review our electricity facts, Shana," Molly suggested when she finished her last carrot. "We still have about ten minutes before science."

I'll need ten days, Meg wanted to say, but no one would believe that right then Meg Milano couldn't tell the positive from the negative end of a battery.

Molly directed the girls to the last empty bench in the sunny courtyard. While Meg searched through her jammed backpack for the all-important science review sheet, Molly lectured the other girls. "Meg and I are going to draw batteries and light bulbs, then you guys have to draw the lines showing how the electricity passes through."

"How shocking!" Stevie joked.

"Revolting!" Laura answered the way they always did when the boring subject of electricity came up.

"You ready, Meg?" Molly asked. "Here's a piece of paper."

Meg held the paper but didn't do anything with it. She *couldn't* do anything with it. Right at that moment she wasn't sure she could even turn on a light switch let alone draw the wires that ran underneath one.

"What's the matter, Meg?" Laura said, sounding worried.

"I don't know where Mr. Retz's handout is," Meg said glumly. "Not that it matters. I forgot to do it." Meg sat on the bench like an old rag doll, her long legs dangling in front of her. Molly was the one standing in front of the group now, study sheets in hand, ready to whip the Friends 4-Ever troops into shape.

"I gave you the sheet last Thursday, didn't I, Meg?" Shana asked. "I thought I did, anyway.

I saw you put it in a big red notebook."

"It's not your fault, Shana," Meg said, not at all used to having other people keep track of her work. "I had my G.A.S.P. notebook with me Tuesday instead of my regular binder, and now I have that but not the red one, which is where the review sheet is. My stuff is half here and half there, but it's always the wrong half."

"Hey, take my sheet. What difference does it make? You're so smart you can figure it out just by looking at it once, anyway," Stevie told Meg to make her feel better.

Meg not only didn't feel better, she felt several degrees worse. Just looking at the sheet for a few minutes wasn't going to help her do the kind of Meg Milano A+ Super Special Job she usually did.

"Why don't you go ahead? I'll borrow Stevie's sheet while you review," Meg said tiredly. She took the paper Stevie held out and went into the building to the empty science room. For four and a half minutes, she tried to cram and jam the information into her brain. It didn't work. When the bell rang, she realized she barely knew the difference between an electrical conductor and a train conductor.

"All *wired* up for the big test, Meg?" Mr. Retzloff joked when he came into the science room. "Or maybe you want to *switch* classes," he added to get her to smile.

Meg smiled, but it was only a 40-watt smile, not the 150-watt special she usually gave her favorite teacher when he kidded her.

"This test is going to be sooo easy," Meg heard next. "Compared to the work in the gifted classes, I mean. I didn't even study for *this*," Erica bragged to Suzi as they breezed by the lab table where even Stevie and Shana were scrunched over their notes.

"I wonder if they're even going to bother taking out a pencil," Meg muttered to Laura.

"Listen up, everybody," Mr. Retzloff said in front of the room. "I hope we have a lot of *live wires* today for this test. Now just take your time. I have plenty of diagrams for you to label and draw, so be careful when you write your answers. Don't rush through." Mr. Retzloff walked to the first lab table with the stack of test sheets. "Any questions before we start?"

Suzi Taylor's hand zoomed up.

"Yes, Suzi?" Mr. Retzloff said, not quite able to conceal a sigh.

"If we finish early, can Erica and I go talk in the nature corner? I have to catch up on some of the astronomy problems I have in my Gifted classes. Plus Erica and I need to talk about *The Gifted Express* newspaper."

Stevie held up two fingers. "Suzi must be slipping," she whispered to Meg. "She only used the *G* word twice."

"Well, there are no extra points for finishing early, Suzi, so I recommend using the entire time for the test," Mr. Retzloff advised. "This goes for all of you. If you do finish early, you can stay in your seats and read, but I have to keep a lid on the talking until everyone finishes."

The Know-It-Alls sighed so loudly, Meg thought the gas was escaping from the Bunsen burners on one of the lab tables. "You can start now. Save plenty of time for the last two questions."

Like everyone else, Meg knew Mr. Retz wasn't the greatest artist in the world, so his light bulb drawings didn't look very bulby, and his batteries looked like rectangular submarines. Still, she couldn't figure out one single diagram on the test. Worse, the old Liberia-Nigeria problem came back, too, when she couldn't tell series circuits from parallel ones.

Let's see, series means more than one, she thought, trying to use some everyday Meg Milano logic to get her through this part of the test. She answered *series* next to all the questions that had to do with more than one battery, one bulb, or one wire. In very un-Meglike fashion she wrote out her answers as lightly as possible. Maybe Mr. Retz wouldn't be able to read her test and she could take a makeup when she was better prepared.

Whenever that might be.

Pausing between the front half and the back half of the test, Meg looked around the table to see how her friends were coming along. Molly's nose was about a half an inch from her paper, and she was gripping her pencil as if she expected a thief to grab it at any minute. Laura's face seemed to be all scrunched eyebrows as she held the sheet away from herself to review her answers. Shana was chewing on her eraser, and Stevie was doodling.

There was no gripping, squinting, chewing, doodling, or worrying over at the Know-It-Alls' table. Meg could see that Erica and Suzi were completely done. In fact, they had actually brought their tests up to Mr. Retzloff's desk. Both of them had their big red Gifted Program binders opened and were doing their best to pretend they weren't even in Crispin Landing Elementary School. Erica gave Meg a big, phony smile when she caught her staring.

There was something about Erica's smile that filled Meg with doubts about *series* and *circuits* all over again. She turned her paper over and changed most of her answers.

"Time's up, gang!" Mr. Retzloff called out. "Everybody done?"

Meg wasn't about to ask for a few extra minutes' time in front of the whole class, so she turned in her paper, mistakes and all. It was over, and so was her reputation as a queen of the brains.

"There are five more minutes before the bell," Mr. Retz said to the class, "so you can let off a little steam and talk 'til the end of the period. Not real steam, of course."

"Whew," Laura said, looking pretty red-faced and scraggly-haired for a change. "I wish Mr. Retzloff wasn't my favorite teacher. Then I could be mad at him for giving such a hard test."

Before Meg could feel relief that someone else found the test so tough, she heard Suzi call out a question to Mr. Retzloff. "Mr. Retzloff, Mr. Retzloff! If I get the bonus question right, does that mean I might get *more* than a hundred on the test? I mean, is it even possible to get, like say, a hundred and ten points or something?" Suzi Taylor asked in her loudest, flirtiest voice.

"Let's see how everybody does on the main part of the test, okay, Suzi?" Mr. Retz answered calmly.

"Maybe she'll get a thousand points or maybe a million," Stevie said, doing a perfect imitation of Suzi's high-pitched voice. "Maybe she'll be in the *Guinness Book of World Records*! This is just the beginning!"

"Give me a break," Shana said in disgust.

"Quiet," Meg hissed. "They're right behind you."

Sure enough, the two Know-It-Alls, stretching themselves as tall as they could when they walked toward the Friends 4-Ever table, swept by as if they were on their way to a parade. "Really, I'm so glad we don't have to be around these *juveniles* every day," Erica said, her backpack nearly conking Laura in the head as she and Suzi left the science room.

"I do not know how you stand them," Molly said to Meg. "My mom's always giving me talks about silver linings when something bad happens. Horseback riding was supposed to be the silver lining for moving to Kansas, and I guess not having to hear those two every day is the silver lining for not getting into the Gifted Program. Poor you."

"My silver lining is you guys," Meg said.

"And, I guess, being picked in the first place. At the end of the year we get to be in the Mental Gymnastics, and it might be on television," Meg added, not at all enthusiastic about talking in front of the whole wide world.

"It's so weird," Stevie said, looking very puzzled. "Until you got into G.A.S.P. I never thought of brains as being something you could exercise or be in contests with. I just thought my brain was a three-pound blob with a skull around it I could use to do head shots in soccer."

"That is sooo gross, Stevie," Laura said. "The Gifted Program is like my ballet and your soccer and Molly's horseback riding. No different."

Meg wanted to hug Laura right then for making what Meg was doing as important as what everyone else was doing. "Thanks, Laura. Once I catch up and get more organized, I think I'll like it. I just have to figure out how to put up with those two. I think they must have somebody doing their work for them. Did you see the way they finished their tests early?"

Everyone stopped by Molly's locker while she fiddled with her lock. "Well, in a way it wasn't as hard as I thought," Molly said. "There was only one question about *parallel* circuits, and all the other answers were *series* circuits."

Meg felt her heart land somewhere down near

the floor. "Isn't it the other way? I mean, *series* means more than one, doesn't it?"

"In electricity, *series* means in a row," Molly told Meg without a shred of doubt in her voice. "If one Christmas tree bulb goes out in a series circuit they all go out. The more expensive kind has two wires parallel, side by side, so even if one bulb burns out, the electricity goes around the burnt-out one, and the other ones light up anyway. You were the one who gave me that tip, Meg, don't you remember?"

"I remember now," Meg groaned. "I think I just got half my test wrong."

"You probably didn't," Laura said, but Meg was too busy kicking herself to hear her friend's comforting words.

"C'mon, Meg, forget it. You'll make it up with your science project and some other tests. There's one on air pressure next week," Molly said when she and Stevie headed down the hall for recess.

All Meg heard was *pressure*. She was going to two schools now, but there was still only one Meg Milano to do all the work. "I'll be out in a minute."

When Meg turned around to join her friends, she was face-to-face with Suzi Taylor. "I'm glad I ran into you, Meg," Suzi said, acting as if she hadn't just seen her in science. "I meant to tell you, your *Gifted Express* article on Earth Day is due tomorrow, not Tuesday."

"What?" Meg cried. "You wrote Tuesday on the assignment sheet. I have it here somewhere. I know you said next week."

Suzi tilted her head and did everything but shake a finger at Meg. "Mrs. Dunwoodie changed it yesterday since the school secretary needs two extra days to type it."

Meg had a strong urge to give each of Suzi's dangling earrings a long, hard pull. "Then why didn't you tell me yesterday?"

"I tried to," Suzi said, "but you and Mr. Wizard were too busy writing notes to each other to listen. Well, now you know."

The recess bell rang, but Meg knew there wasn't going to be any recess for her. She gathered up her things, some from her regular classes and a huge pile from G.A.S.P., then went into the classroom. She pushed two desks together and slammed down books, papers, two binders, and a handful of purple teacher handouts.

She was going to organize her life.

First, she opened up the red Gifted and Special Program binder. Into one section, she put her notes and papers for *The Gifted Express*. Except, of course, for Suzi's assignment sheet, which she crumpled into a ball and pitched into the waste-basket. In a few minutes, her Crispin Landing Elementary life was in one small neat pile of papers and books. Her G.A.S.P. pile, much taller, was in another. Now if she could only keep them straight.

After weeding out some old homework sheets she didn't need anymore, Meg came to her supply of kitten stationery. Which pile did that belong to? She didn't know. Pulling a fresh sheet from the top, she began to write:

FRIENDS 4-EVER CHECK-OFF
APOLOGY SHEET

Dear Everybody,

Remember when all my letters were PAGES and PAGES long? I wish this one could be, but I only have a few minutes before you get back. Please check off the right box, then pass it on to the next person.

☐ *I'm sorry about not tutoring you for the math test.*

☐ *I'm sorry I didn't review* **pygmy** *with you.*

☐ *I'm sorry I forgot about planning the Easter egg hunt.*

☐ *I'm sorry I didn't say thanks for being so understanding.*

See you when the jelly fishes,

Meg

FOUR MINUS ONE
EQUALS THREE

"Meg! Meg! Breakfast. Come on downstairs!" Meg could hear her parents' footsteps overhead as they crisscrossed the kitchen floor. Two creaks meant someone was opening the refrigerator. Half a creak was probably her dad shifting one foot to the other in front of the stove while he waited for his coffee to drip into the pot.

"Meg! You up?" Mrs. Milano called.

"No, I'm down," Meg shouted up the cellar stairs.

"So that explains why Marmalade's lying here like an overgrown beanbag instead of wrapping himself around my legs for food," Mr. Milano said. "I thought maybe he decided to start his diet today. Looks like Meg already fed him, Diane."

Meg's parents didn't realize how clearly the sound traveled from the kitchen straight into the cellar where Meg was packing up her Future City building to bring to G.A.S.P. Her mother was whispering to her dad, but every word was loud and clear. "She's been getting up earlier every day. I'm really beginning to wonder if this Gifted Program is too much for her, Peter. She's got circles under her eyes. And last night she fell asleep in her clothes."

Meg ripped off a strip of masking tape from the dispenser on the workbench. So now her parents didn't think she could handle the Gifted Program *and* regular school? She wished they'd make up their minds. First they pushed her to go, and now that she was going, they thought she couldn't stick it out!

"Cocoa's ready," her mother called out.

Warm cocoa. Normally that would have sent Meg zooming into the kitchen, but today her stomach was still up in her bedroom sound asleep and not the least bit interested in hot cocoa. And it would be hard to stay mad at her parents if she gave in and took even one sip of it.

"What? For meeee?" Mr. Milano said in his

silly Pee-wee voice when Meg came upstairs with the brown cardboard box. "It's too early for Christmas, and it's not my birthday."

"You look pretty peaky today, Meg," Mrs. Milano commented when Meg didn't respond to her dad's joke with her usual sunny smile.

"I'm fine," Meg answered, though she would have given anything for her pair of fake eyeball glasses so she could shut her real eyes underneath and go to sleep. She sipped *at* her cocoa, but none of the liquid actually went down. The Cheerios were easier. Marmalade positioned himself next to Meg's right leg, the perfect spot to catch the dry little *o*'s Meg sneaked down from the top of her cereal bowl. In no time, her bowl looked as if a very hungry girl had attacked it.

"More cereal?" Mrs. Milano asked a few minutes later.

"No thanks, Mom. I'm going out to put my project in the car."

After Meg carefully slid her project box into the backseat, she peeked in the fence knothole to see if anyone had made a Friends 4-Ever delivery during the night. Lately, it seemed, she and her friends wrote to each other more than they talked. Sure enough, there was a note from Molly. But when Meg began to read she noticed the message wasn't to her at all. It was for Laura!

Dear Laura,

Don't forget our secret meeting at recess today. We've got to finish talking about F.F.E.R.P. Whatever you do, don't breathe a word to Meg, if you even see her. She's never around anymore.

Call U when my ear rings,

Molly

Meg reread the note to make sure her sleepy eyes weren't tricking her. Yes, the note was for Laura. Molly must have put it in Meg's mail spot by mistake. And, yes, there in Molly's rainbow writing was "F.F.E.R.P.," the silly code name Stevie had made up months ago for the Friends 4-Ever Rescue Plan. F.F.E.R.P. had been Meg's idea for keeping Molly in Rhode Island instead of going back to Kansas after a Christmas visit. Since the Friends 4-Ever Rescue Plan had worked, who was left to rescue?

"Everything all packed?" Mrs. Milano asked

when she came out to the driveway. Meg nodded, but her mother's chatter barely interrupted her poisonous thoughts about how — once again — Molly Quindlen was copying Meg Milano.

"It takes forever to make a left out of Crispin Landing Road during the rush hour," Mrs. Milano complained, but Meg wasn't thinking about the Camden traffic. Who did Molly think she was, anyway? Meg was in charge of secret meetings, emergency meetings, and rescue plans, not Molly Quindlen!

By the time Mrs. Milano pulled up to the Roger Williams Middle School, Meg had a new name for F.F.E.R.P., the Friends 4-Ever *Return* Plan. Molly could just go right back to Kansas and take her science project and her rainbow notes with her! Or maybe she would name it the Friends 4-Ever Rat Plan or the Friends 4-Ever Revenge Plan. By the time Mrs. Milano drove up to the middle school, Meg had a long list of new F.F.E.R.P. names, none of them very nice.

"Good luck with the project, Meg. Want some help carrying it in?" Mrs. Milano asked. She had no idea what Meg was mumbling about in the backseat.

"Mom! It's only this and my backpack." Even if Meg had to balance the Empire State Building in one hand and the Statue of Liberty in the other, no way was she going to let her mother go with her into the middle school! Honestly, her mother never learned.

Becky Bishop wasn't as lucky. When Meg caught up with Becky, Mrs. Bishop peeked over the top of the incredible silvery structure she was carrying, complete with its own space shuttle. "Oh, hello, Meg. My goodness, we practically need a crane to get this into the building, don't we?"

"No *we* don't, Mom," a very annoyed-looking Becky said. "See? Meg got hers to school by herself."

Mrs. Bishop just kept right on walking down the hall. "Well, darling, after all our hard work, we wouldn't want to take any chances dropping this, now, would we?"

"No, we wouldn't," Becky muttered, making a sour-pickle face behind her mother's back.

"Where should I put this, Mrs. Dunwoodie?" Mrs. Bishop sang out when they got to the G.A.S.P. room.

"Oh, my!" Mrs. Dunwoodie said, breathless with the excitement of having so many gifted architects in *her* class. Right away Meg noticed that not one of the projects but hers could possibly fit into a cardboard box. "Perhaps that corner there," Mrs. Dunwoodie suggested. "I'm afraid we're running out of display space," she added, helping Mrs. Bishop carefully position Becky's project next to what looked like the Kennedy Space Center. Only bigger. "What a creative structure, Becky. So original."

"Thank you." Mrs. Bishop smiled proudly while nudging her elbow into Becky's side.

"Thank you," Becky muttered. "See you later, Mom."

While Mrs. Bishop huddled with Mrs. Dunwoodie, Becky helped Meg find room for her building. "I love it. I just love it, Meg," Becky said admiringly. "What is it?"

"It's the Pencil Palace," Meg said, finally happy that her Future Building was done. "It's made out of a hundred and three pencils glued together. See, in the future everybody'll be using computers and special light-ray pens, so they'll be recycling old-fashioned wooden pencils for other things."

"Verrry gifted," Chris Malone said when he overheard Meg's explanation. "In-genius."

"It's great," Becky said. "At least you can tell *your* parents didn't do your project." When Meg's face clouded over, she added, "That's a compliment, Meg. Look at all these others, including mine. Honestly, I'm going to tell Mrs.

Dunwoodie to put my mom's and dad's names on the grade instead of mine. My mom's hoping for an A plus."

Meg felt a tiny bit better. Although the Pencil Palace looked more like one of the cozy hotels she used to design when she was little and had a few too many sequins, Meg had drawn all the plans and glued together all the pencils herself. Mainly at six o'clock in the morning.

"Where's your project, Chris?" Meg asked when she noticed he didn't seem to be carrying anything but his backpack.

Chris unzipped the front pocket and pulled out a small white box. Lifting the lid, he held out the bottom of the box for the girls to see. "Life in the year three thousand!"

Meg bent her head down for a closer look. Inside was a teeny kitchen with a family of two parents and two kids sitting around the table eating what looked like chocolate chip cookies. Everything was tiny, from the very small clay forms of the humans to the toothpick legs of the kitchen table. Meg, who loved anything minia-ture, practically swooned at the sight of the tiny forks made out of paper clip wire and the small vase in the middle of the table. "I love it." She hesitated. "I hate to say this, but do you think it's futuristic enough?"

This question didn't faze Chris at all. "It's the way humans are going to evolve, you know, change after a long time. Everybody's slowly going to get smaller so we don't have to use up so much air and water. Our great-great-great-great grandchildren are going to be no bigger than ants, but in every other way, they'll be just like us. Fighting over the last cookie."

"Mrs. Dunwoodie's going to throw you out of G.A.S.P.," Becky said without any hesitation.

"She can't. Is this any more unrealistic than *that*?" Chris pointed to the Kennedy Space Center-sized structure next to Becky's. It was Suzi Taylor's project, or rather Mrs. Taylor's project by the looks of it. "I mean, what'd she do, get a NASA engineer to build it?"

"Well, no NASA engineer built *that* one," Erica said when she stopped in front of Meg's Pencil Palace. "Whoever did that must have mixed up their *real* project with their little brother's nursery school exhibit."

Meg was steaming, and she turned to Becky and Chris for help. Unfortunately, her two friends had begun one of their daily morning arguments. Becky and Chris had been friends practically since *birth* and had the same kinds of fights Meg had often seen Stevie have with her brothers — whiny arguments that went on for ever. They were having one now, with Chris insisting he would take Mrs. Dunwoodie to the Supreme Court if she didn't think his project was futuristic enough.

Without Chris or Becky to say something funny about the Know-It-Alls, Meg's Pencil Palace began to look more and more babyish the longer she looked at it. Did she really have to spell out "Pencil Palace" with purple glitter glue? And why on earth had she stuck a small plastic bear at the top or decorated the foundation with stickers? Another Meg Milano Mess.

"*Jeopardy* Time! *Jeopardy* Time!" Mrs. Dunwoodie's announcement caused the usual cheers and chair scraping that always followed those words. Next to Mock Trials, *Jeopardy* Time was also Super Show-off Time, and one of Meg's, Becky's, and Chris's least favorite G.A.S.P. activities.

"Oh, no," Becky grumbled. "I can't believe we have *Jeopardy* AND our projects in one day."

Like everyone in the room, Meg picked up her chair and brought it to the back where most of the G.A.S.P. kids had already set up their chairs in rows. Becky, Meg, and Chris squeezed themselves and their chairs past the Know-It-Alls and way behind the Roaring Brook bigmouths who were arranging their chairs in the front row.

Mrs. Dunwoodie was the host of the show and displayed an embarrassing homemade sign in the shape of a television set. On the screen she had drawn the words, *The Gifted and Special Program Presents: Jeopardy!*

"Today our first category will be World History Before 1600," Mrs. Dunwoodie announced.

Chris turned to Becky and Meg, pulled down his lower eyelids, and stuck out his tongue. By the sound of all the grumbles and complaints, World History Before 1600 wasn't a big favorite with the front-row geniuses, either.

Meg scrunched herself down as low as she could without sliding off her chair. But since Mrs. Dunwoodie had X-ray vision and could see right through Josh Alexander, Meg's blobby posture didn't do any good. "Meg, would you come up and sit on my right, please?" the G.A.S.P. director called out. "And I think I'll have, mmm, let's see, Erica on my left."

While Mrs. Dunwoodie shuffled her question cards, which always took forever, Erica mouthed something to Suzi that looked to Meg like, "My parents gave me three hundred dollars to spend on lunch." Erica and Suzi never missed a chance to let the class know that *their* parents had given *them* permission to eat lunch off the school grounds like real middle schoolers. Except for two Roaring Brook students who also had brothers and sisters in the middle school, most of the G.A.S.P. kids had to eat lunch in the cafeteria and only *hear* about the French fries at the Yellow Brick Road and how it was hard to finish their Double Devil Hot Fudge Sundaes.

Mrs. Dunwoodie held up the first card and put an end to Erica and Suzi's "conversation." On the card, Mrs. Dunwoodie had scrawled out: *The famous Queen of Egypt who fell in love with Marc Anthony.*

Who was Cleopatra? Meg answered correctly in her head, but unfortunately now it was Erica's turn.

"Who was Cleopatra, of course," Erica said as if Mrs. Dunwoodie had asked her who was Humpty-Dumpty.

"A good start, Erica. Now, Meg, here's your card." Mrs. Dunwoodie held up a card that only had three words: *English Civil Rights.*

Meg looked out at Chris and Becky who both had sympathetic expressions for Meg, but no answers written on their foreheads.

"What is the Bill of Rights?" Meg guessed, but Mrs. Dunwoodie shook her head and flashed the card at Erica.

"What is the Magna Carta?" Erica answered as if she'd written the document herself.

When Meg got back to her seat, Becky whispered just the right thing: "What a Know-It-All! And you know why? Part of that trip she won to Washington was to go to the National Library or Archives, whatever it's called, and there's a copy of the Magna whatever there. I heard Suzi bragging about it to Josh. You'd think they won a trip to Paris or something."

The *Jeopardy* contest went on, and as usual the same few kids won the same few prizes, coupons for free ice-cream sandwiches in the cafeteria. Erica and Suzi always refused them since they ate their lunches *in town*. The week before they'd actually had the nerve to offer their coupons to Meg who hated the middle school's cardboardy ice-cream sandwiches.

The only good thing about getting knocked out so early, Meg thought, was not having to worry about her turn coming up. Now she could daydream or doodle or write notes to Chris and Becky or to her other friends. If she still had any, that is.

As she sat only half listening to kids identify everything from pharaohs to knights, Meg crumpled and uncrumpled Molly's note to Laura. Her almost brand-new G.A.S.P. watch said ten o'clock. Did she know where the Friends 4-Ever were? Unfortunately she had a pretty good idea. At that very moment, Meg could picture the three of them in the Crispin Landing Elementary playground tunnel having a secret meeting. For a change they wouldn't have to scrunch themselves up the way they did when Meg was there. Today, it was Friends 4-Ever, minus one.

7

THE FRIENDS 4-EVER
RESCUE PLAN II

"Meg, phone again! It's Molly," Mrs. Milano called from downstairs. "Did you win a contest or something? The phone hasn't stopped ringing since you got home!"

Thank goodness for that, Meg thought to herself. After delivering her notes on the way home from the bus stop, Meg had waited by the phone. And waited. When no one called by three-thirty, she actually went back to Laura's, Stevie's, and Molly's mail spots and rechecked each one to make sure her notes hadn't blown away. But the notes were untouched, and there was no sign of her friends. Were they having *another* secret meeting someplace?

Thirty long minutes later the phone finally rang, with a puzzled Laura, and fifteen minutes later with a puzzled Stevie, calling. Both of them asked Meg what the big emergency was all about. "Just come," Meg answered mysteriously. How could she tell them that never seeing her friends anymore *was* an emergency?

Now Molly would want to know the same thing. Meg carried her parents' phone from their bedroom and stretched the cord across the hallway to her own room.

"Hi, it's me," Molly said. "I just got home and found your note in my hammock. What's up, Meg? Is something the matter?"

"I just wanted to have a meeting, that's all," Meg answered. "We haven't had one at my house for ages, so I planned one for tonight."

"What's the big emergency, I mean?" Molly asked. "See, we were going to have a real meeting at my house Friday night, after pizza, if you — "

"If what, Molly? If I don't have to go to an *opera* again or do homework? Well, maybe you can just have it without me if I can't come. You probably have lots of meetings without me."

Meg could hear breathing on the other end of the phone for so long she wasn't sure Molly wanted to talk anymore. But then she said, "Are

103

we still having a fight, Meg?" Molly sounded hurt and confused. "We clinked beakers, remember?"

Meg swallowed hard. "Can you just come over, Molly? Please."

"I think my parents will let me if I say we're working on our science projects, okay?"

"Okay."

And the Meg Milano Project, too, Meg thought.

After she put the phone back in her parents' room, Meg returned to her own room. "Who'd want to come to a meeting in a Dumpster?" she said to the piles of books on her desk, the overflowing wastebasket, and the Friends 4-Ever Post Office poster that was hanging sideways from her door by one piece of tape. "Not me, that's for sure."

This did not look like the official Friends 4-Ever headquarters. What with the Pencil Palace, the science project, learning about electrical circuits, and trying not to get knocked out too early in the weekly *Jeopardy* match, Meg's orderly room had somehow turned into a mushroom-growing sort of place.

"I can't have everybody see this!" she said, squashing down the papers in the wastebasket with her right foot. "I have to set an example."

She squashed more papers down with her left foot. After all, wasn't Stevie always kidding her about how she lined up her pencils in the same direction and color coded her T-shirts? And what sort of person would leave paper clips just lying all over instead of arranging them in their own special tray? Certainly not the founder of Friends 4-Ever.

Forgetting about all the schoolwork she had to do — and shoving the awful red G.A.S.P. binder out of sight — Meg took a deep breath. First she put on her painter's pants, so she would have plenty of pockets for sorting out the 'N Stuff rocks, rings, acorns, and stray stickers that had been reproducing all over her room for the last few weeks.

"I wonder if there's still a desk under here." Meg lifted the stacks of books covering her desk and spread them out on the floor. Though she was awfully tempted to reread the creepy pages of *The Clue in the Jewel Box*, she put the Nancy Drew book in the K pile, grouping each book by author just the way Mrs. Silver, the school librarian, had shown the class.

When her desk was finally clear, Meg looked at her watch and allowed herself a thirty-second break to admire all the snapshots of her friends she had arranged under the glass top of the desk.

"Mmm, almost time for Pet Washing Day," she said out loud when she saw a photo of Stevie trying to hold on to Molly's dog, a very sudsy-looking Riggs, a couple of years before. She opened the desk drawer, not yet too mush-roomy, and pulled out her Friends 4-Ever Things to Do checklist. This was a joke birthday gift from Stevie, but Meg took it very seriously. On the top line she filled in: *Pet Washing Day???* so she would remember to bring it up at the meeting first thing.

"So *there's* my whistle!" Meg said when she moved the desk away from the wall to see if any treasures had fallen back there. Now, with her Things to Do checklist and the whistle around her neck, she was complete.

"Whoa, what's all this?" Mrs. Milano cried when she came upstairs and saw Meg in the middle of the cleanup.

"My room's a mess," Meg explained, "so I decided to straighten it out."

Mrs. Milano smiled. "I was getting worried about you when I noticed a Nancy Drew book mixed in with your rock-collecting books. I almost took your temperature."

"I know, Mom, I know. I'm straightening out all my books this afternoon *and* my 'N' Stuff box *and* my sock drawer," Meg announced. "I found a bathing suit in there when I was getting ready for school this morning."

"Call the police!" Mrs. Milano joked, happy to see Meg enjoying one of her favorite pastimes — organizing.

Meg hated to stop making her piles of this and that, but she couldn't help noticing the book her mother was carrying, the mustard-colored, dreaded, *Wordly Wise.* "Oh, no, tomorrow's Thursday!"

"*Wordly Wise* day. We'd better get started reviewing." Mrs. Milano paused when she noticed Meg's smile was now a frown. "Well, we don't have to review the questions right this minute. I suppose we could do it after dinner."

"No we can't," Meg wailed. "I'm having a Friends 4-Ever meeting tonight! That's why everybody was calling up before."

Mrs. Milano did not do a very good job of hiding the frown on her own face. "Now, Meg," she began, "I'll try not to get mad about having a meeting without telling me, but we did work out this study schedule after what happened on that electricity test. That's what you wanted to do, remember?"

Meg nodded, though she did not want to remember anything of the kind. She knew exactly what her mother was talking about. In fact, at that very moment, about a hundred pieces of the famous electricity test were lying squashed at the very bottom of Meg's wastebasket so that she would never again have to see a C-minus next to the name Meg Milano.

"Look, there isn't really enough time to finish your room *and* your schoolwork. I certainly don't think your friends will mind about your room," Mrs. Milano pointed out. "Why don't you see how far you get studying your vocabulary and answering the history questions you told me about? Then maybe later I can help you review."

"But, Mom. Nothing's set up for the meeting. There's no place to even sit," Meg whined, the energy going out of her a little at a time.

"It's up to you," Mrs. Milano said before finally leaving. *It's up to you* always sounded to Meg as if her mother left something out, such as *if you want to ruin your life*.

Meg did her best to ignore the mess. If she started working on her homework right away, maybe she *could* get it done before everyone came over. Picking up *Wordly Wise*, she turned to page fifty-seven, which began with the word *burden: anything carried that is too heavy; something that weighs on one's mind.* Meg had a ton weighing on her mind, but maybe working hard for the next couple hours would help her get rid of the weight.

Tap. Tap, tap. Tap. When Meg heard the Friends 4-Ever secret knock at seven sharp, she got up from her desk where she had been answering questions about the French and Indian War.

"We're here!" Stevie announced. She bounded in without waiting for Meg to open the door. Looking around Meg's room, Stevie's eyes opened wide. "Hey, I guess we're not here. This looks just like my room."

Meg could see the same shocked expressions on Laura's and Molly's faces, too. None of them had been up in Meg's room since she had started her G.A.S.P. classes. *This* room was definitely not the Meg Milano room they had last seen.

This was a C-minus room.

"Is your room the emergency?" Laura asked, looking a little nervous about her question.

"If it is, then you'd better call an ambulance," Stevie joked, but nobody laughed.

Meg pushed back a curl that was itching her forehead. "It's not illegal to have a messy room."

"Or I'd be in jail and — " Stevie began until Molly jabbed her in the ribs.

"So what *is* the emergency, Meg?" Molly wanted to know. "We *can* clean your room *or* work on our projects together. We left our science stuff down in the cellar when we came in."

"I just wanted to have a normal meeting for a change."

Laura, Stevie, and Molly looked at each other with the same question on their faces: *This* was Meg's big emergency?

Meg blew her whistle the way she always did to start a meeting, but it didn't have the usual effect. The girls kept milling around the room, picking up her books, looking through the odds and ends scattered on her dresser, and studying the photo collage on her desk. Had it been so long, they didn't know the whistle signaled the start of a meeting?

Meg blew the whistle again, but the second time only a peep of air came out. Laura, Stevie, and Molly went right on dawdling as if they didn't even *want* the meeting to start.

"Hey, guys, I know it's been a long time, but in case you didn't notice I just blew the whistle to start the meeting." But the only thing that was starting up was Meg's temper.

The girls sat down, but they didn't *settle* down the way they were supposed to when a meeting began. Stevie was trying out different knots on her high-tops. Laura was doing some kind of ballet flexing with her right leg. And Molly sat on the floor shifting around and looking uncomfortable.

Meg had a feeling that they were about to announce something terrible. Was someone else moving away? Were they getting a new fourth person to replace Meg in Friends 4-Ever — someone who wasn't always so busy with Pencil Palaces and geography bees?

She had to take charge of the meeting, she just had to, before they said something she didn't want to hear. If everyone saw that she was back to normal again, running things and having great ideas just like before, they would think twice about dropping her.

"Laura, could you take attendance?" Meg said, trying hard to make her voice steady and strong.

"Um, yeah, but I forgot my Friends 4-Ever notebook for the meeting. Um, Stevie?"

"Here."

"Meg?"

"Here."

"Molly?"

Silence. "Come in, come in, Molly," Laura said.

"Oh, I'm here," Molly said, though she seemed to Meg to be far away.

Just keep going. Mention the Pet Wash, Meg coached herself. "How about doing the Crispin Landing Pet Wash now that it's getting warmer?" she finally asked. But from everyone's expressions, she might as well have said, "Why don't we all study spelling or do seventy-five push-ups?"

When no one answered, Meg didn't know what to do next. How could she? Lately she hadn't had five spare minutes to think up anything fun or new that would make her friends look happy that they were having a real meeting at last.

"Never mind," Meg said about the Pet Wash. "Maybe we should just work on our science projects like we told our parents."

Molly looked at Laura, and Laura looked at Stevie. "I know you wanted this meeting, Meg," Molly said. "But I — I mean we — we think we want to bring up something else first."

Meg twisted her whistle but didn't say anything. She hoped they were going to tell her about the secret meeting, so it wouldn't be a secret anymore.

"See, we had this secret meeting today, kind of our own emergency meeting, in the playground tunnel at recess," Molly began. "We only had twenty minutes, but we spent the whole time talking about you."

"You did?"Meg asked, not quite sure whether what Molly was going to say was going to make her feel better or worse.

"We think it's time for another Friends 4-Ever Rescue Plan," Molly announced.

"Son of F.F.E.R.P.!" Stevie blurted out.

While Meg wondered what this was all about, Laura spoke up. "We never see you anymore. All we've had lately are notes, not you. Your schedule is worse than ever. You can only talk on the phone about two minutes a day between projects and compositions and all the other stuff you have to do. Things haven't been the same lately. And we figured out why. *You* haven't been the same lately."

These words — these true words — made Meg feel heavy and sad. She felt — *burdened*. She had let her friends down. She knew what was coming next, she just knew it. Her friends were going to drop her.

"You look so unhappy all the time," Laura continued. "Remember the other day when we caught up with you after you got off the middle school bus?"

Meg nodded.

"Well, you were walking funny, not the way you usually do, you know, skipping and bouncing like something fun is just waiting for you to get it started." Laura looked at Molly for help. "Am I explaining this right?"

Molly nodded. "Good so far."

Laura continued on. "Anyway, you were dragging down Doubletree Court, and the strap of your backpack was kind of dangling behind you on the ground. We didn't even know it was you at first until we caught up! You just didn't look like the same old Meg."

Meg felt tears forming behind her eyeballs, but she didn't cry. In fact, she almost smiled when she thought of a funny coincidence. "You know what's weird? Do you want to know what's incredibly weird? I found the note you wrote to Laura, Molly. The one this morning about your secret meeting? So *I* decided *I* had to have a meeting to prove I am still the same old me."

"And an official genius besides," Stevie interrupted.

Meg went on. "Only while I was getting ready for you guys to come over, I said to myself, 'Margaret Milano, you are not the same old you. Your room's a mess and so are you! All you do is run around trying to keep up with G.A.S.P. and regular school.' "

"Good thing we didn't walk in while you were saying all that to nobody," Stevie broke in.

"Anyway, I realized I hate it! I cannot stand being in this program where every day is like the geography bee. I guess I'm just not gifted enough."

"But that's just it, Meg, you are!" Molly cried. "Only *we* need your gifts. We miss them."

"We haven't done one fun thing since you started G.A.S.P.," Stevie complained.

"Neither have I,"Meg said, getting herself into a Meg Milano tizzy. "I do like some of the things they do at the program, and I made friends with Chris and Becky, but there's not enough time to have fun anymore. Plus Mrs. Dunwoodie makes everything into a big contest. I think I hate that the most."

"You're just not like that," Laura agreed.

"Weeell, sometimes she is," Stevie said until Molly gave her another rib jabbing. "What I mean is, you know how to think up stuff like our different clubs and get us all organized for geography bees and science projects so that we don't flunk school. But you never seem to like it when it's actually happening."

Meg nodded. "You are so right, Stevie! That's me every time. *The Magic Princess*. The time I started soccer but hated it when we had to play games against other teams. The dumb geography bee. I guess I just like doing the stuff but not the part where you have to get up in front of everybody, and people are looking at you." Meg paused. "Maybe someday I'll be okay about that, but you're sure right about me, guys." Meg stopped to take a breath. "It's just too bad I have five more weeks of G.A.S.P. left. I don't think I can stand it."

Molly's eyes were bright and her cheeks red with excitement. "Maybe you don't have to stand it. After recess today, I overheard Mrs. Courtney, the principal, say a couple kids weren't finishing the whole eight weeks because they were getting behind in regular school."

Meg wondered who that was. Except for Chris and Becky, everybody else just bragged and bragged about being in G.A.S.P. and sailed through all the work as if they were learning the alphabet.

"I thought about quitting, then I made myself

stop thinking about it," Meg told her friends. "I know this is a dumb reason for staying in G.A.S.P., but I don't think I could stand having Erica and Suzi learn that I dropped out."

"Well, we all know Suzi and Erica wouldn't quit," Stevie muttered. "They'd go bald before they ever quit something that has the word 'gifted' in front of it."

Laura and Molly laughed at Stevie's joke and tried to picture the Know-It-Alls without their silly bangs. While they giggled, Meg thought and thought.

"I'm just not a quitter," Meg went on. "Or a loser."

"No way!" Stevie cried. "You're a joiner, an organizer, a coach, a starter-upper."

"Except I never have time to do those things." Meg said.

"Quitting G.A.S.P. doesn't mean you're a quitter or a loser," Molly observed. "If you're gifted, you're gifted even if you aren't in G.A.S.P."

"You know what? Ever since I started in the Gifted Program, I haven't felt one bit smart. Plus I goofed up in Mr. Retzloff's — my best class! Even though I got picked for G.A.S.P. I've been feeling like a loser."

"We know! We know," all three girls cried.

"That's why we had our meeting. We want to rescue you from G.A.S.P.," Molly said, "like you rescued me from Kansas."

Meg's wheels were turning fast now. "You don't need to rescue me. I'm going to rescue myself. I'll talk to my mom and dad about leaving G.A.S.P. — for now, anyway. My mom's been saying I don't get enough sleep anymore and that I'm getting bags under my eyes. Am I?"

"Yup, you are." Stevie made circles with her fingers around her eyes and looked like a baggy-eyed raccoon.

"I'll mention it to my parents tonight," Meg went on. "After Shampoo Time and *Wordly Wise*, of course."

"Ugh," everybody groaned at the same time.

"I guess we can cross F.F.E.R.P. off our list, right, Meg?" Stevie said with a laugh.

"You bet," Meg answered. "And I'll cross this out for now." She held up her Things to Do checklist. "We've got to get organized here. Before we can wash the neighborhood pets, we have to finish our science projects."

"Oh, no, she's back," Stevie groaned. "General Milano is back."

Meg blew on her whistle, and this time everyone sat at attention. "Come on now, troops.

118

Down to the basement. Left, right, left, right," she barked. "We have lots to do, and we'd better get going."

Stevie saluted Meg. "Stephanie Ames reporting for duty," she said.

Laura and Molly fell into line, and everyone marched down the stairs to see what was next on Meg's list.

THE LAST G.A.S.P.

"Would somebody please tell me why it always rains whenever we have to transport these projects to school?" Mr. Milano grumbled. While Meg and her mother carefully balanced the now-completed science project, Mr. Milano held open a humongous black trash bag.

"Daddy, watch out for my cliff! It won't fit," Meg cried when the bag bunched up near the middle of the project.

"Whew, let's put it down," Mrs. Milano suggested. "Meg's right, it won't fit into one of these bags, Peter. Why don't I cut out a piece of that old shower curtain, and we'll cover the whole thing with that?"

Carefully Meg and her mother walked the project back to the workbench and set it down gently.

"It's quite a masterpiece," Mrs. Milano said, softly stroking the model cliff that overlooked the model town. "You sure did a great job, Meg, a hard job. And I have to confess I'm glad you didn't let me and Dad interfere too much. You've been super about getting this together on your own. Dad and I have been swamped with work lately. You're just getting so grown-up," Mrs. Milano sighed, giving Meg a hug.

Now. Ask them now, Meg told herself.

For two days she had been waiting for the perfect time to bring up the subject of dropping out of G.A.S.P. But until today, her parents had been too busy with work to be in the kind of relaxed mood Meg wanted them to be in when she dropped the bomb.

"Thanks, Mom," Meg said. "I *am* glad I finished it myself."

"You're just getting so independent," Mr. Milano said, sounding happy and sad at the same time. "Going off to the middle school for those special classes, keeping up with all your work."

Uh-oh. Maybe now isn't a good time, either, Meg thought. She could just picture their beaming smiles crumbling right in front of her. On

121

the other hand, she reasoned, better to tell them when they're in a good mood.

"About the classes," Meg began, "Mrs. Courtney said two kids are dropping out."

Mrs. Milano's eyebrows shot up. "Do you know who they are, Meg? I wonder what the problem is. I suppose too much work, judging by how little sleep you're getting these days."

"And not seeing my friends," Meg threw in.

Mr. Milano stopped measuring the old plastic shower curtain. "You know, I miss the racket. I *actually* miss the racket of those kids rumbling up and down our stairs, wearing out our lawn, and emptying our refrigerator."

Mrs. Milano sighed. "I had to throw out some Chiparoos yesterday because they'd gone stale from no one devouring them. Usually we run out two days before it's time to go grocery shopping. I guess you girls will catch up this summer, or maybe after the science fair is over."

This was the moment. Meg just knew it. "Or maybe sooner, Mom."

Now Mrs. Milano's eyebrows rose again.

"I was thinking of leaving G.A.S.P., too," Meg began. "Even when the science fair is over, I still have my Abigail Adams report to do, and Stevie's been bugging me about doing soccer again when the season starts, and — "

"You need a break?" Mr. Milano said, forgetting all about the rainy day and the geology project they had to get to the school gym in a little while.

"I hate G.A.S.P.," Meg confessed. "I only like some of the kids, but Mrs. Dunwoodie always makes everything a big race. Monday we even had to analyze vitamins and stuff in the school lunch! We couldn't just eat it like normal kids."

When Meg's parents smiled, she knew this was a good time to press on. "We have to go to another opera in two weeks, and it's the same night as Molly's birthday. And I have two book reports due the same week and . . ."

Meg could practically see two mothers struggling inside her mom's head. One Mrs. Milano was probably saying how important it is to finish what you start. The other Mrs. Milano was probably saying how unhealthy it is not to get enough sleep or enjoy your life.

Mrs. Milano looked at Meg for an awfully long time and ran a finger under each of Meg's eyes. "I do hate seeing these baggy eyes, Meg. You haven't been a rested girl lately, and we haven't had even one afternoon together since I don't know when."

"February twentieth," Meg blurted out.

Mrs. Milano burst out laughing. "You're probably exaggerating, but only a little. I wish I weren't such a stickler about finishing what you start."

"What about this?" Meg flung her hand out over the science project. "I finished this. And I made the finals for the geography bee. I just wasn't so hot on figuring out how much fat was in the chicken patties at the middle school Monday."

"And you won't have to again, Mego," Mr. Milano said firmly. "I think you should quit."

Mrs. Milano was still thinking, Meg could see. "I suppose there's a lesson in all this. I mean about taking a second look at our decisions."

"Oh, Mom!" Meg groaned, but she was smiling when she said it. "Does that mean if I learn that lesson, I can quit G.A.S.P.?"

"I . . . I think so," Mrs. Milano said without even a tiny frown. "Now let's get this thing in the car before I change my mind."

When Quitting Day came, Meg couldn't believe how great she felt. How great did she feel? Meg Milano felt so great she gave her hair a quick comb without even checking for boingies!

"No black today." She pushed back one hanger after another in her closet until she came to the red suspender skirt. Pulling it over a white T-shirt, she began singing.

Still humming, she bounced down the stairs two at a time and landed with a crash. Terrified by this unexpected noise so early in the morning, Marmalade skidded across the wooden hallway floor until the magazine rack in the living room stopped him from landing in the next state.

"That's the most exercise he's going to get all day," Mr. Milano observed as he came down the stairs one at a time without bouncing or crashing at the bottom. "Wonder where the delivery guy threw my paper today," he said on his way out to search for his morning newspaper. "Up in a tree? In a puddle? Or maybe I'll get real lucky and find it under the car, and I can change the oil at the same time."

"Oh, Daddy." Meg sighed the way she always did when her dad made these exaggerated comments every morning. Meg couldn't imagine why grown-ups needed coffee and newspapers first thing every day, but they did.

When Meg walked into the kitchen, her mother took a long, slow sip from her coffee mug. "Morning, Meg," she said before taking another sip. "The red skirt looks adorable with that T-shirt."

"Thanks, Mom. What's for breakfast?"

"Depends. Fruit and muffins if you take the bus, pancakes if you want a ride with me. I'm dropping off this month's newsletter at the printer's. I'll be going right by the middle school. So what'll it be?"

Meg tried to decide about breakfast and about the ride. In the week that had passed since her parents agreed that leaving the Gifted Program might be a good idea, she'd been afraid her parents were secretly disappointed.

She was still thinking hard when her mother looked up from her coffee cup and smiled. "You know, it's going to be nice having you around and not so busy after today. My newsletter on plaque control is done now, so I'm going to have a little more time, too. Maybe we can go into town next week and get you bigger sneakers and see if the yarn store has some new colored string for your friendship bracelets."

"Can we do that?" Meg asked. It had been ages since she and her mother had had time to do anything except wash hair during Shampoo Time or review for tests during Homework Time. Maybe, for a change, they could have some Do Nothing Time together.

"Let's go Tuesday," her mother answered. "So what do you want for breakfast, anyway?"

"Pancakes, Mom. *And* a ride to school."

"You sure you don't want to take the bus?" her mother asked. "It's your last chance until you get to middle school, you know."

"I know, but now that I've done it, it's not such a big deal. I can wait for a couple of years — when I'm ready."

"Me, too," Mrs. Milano said. "Now, what'll it be? Blueberry or plain pancakes?"

Going into the Roger Williams Middle School was a lot easier on Meg's last day than on her first. The streams of taller, older kids didn't bother her now. Like them, she knew how to find the library, gym, and water fountains. Like them, she had a couple of friends to walk to classes with, too.

"Deserter," Chris Malone teased when he joined Meg in the crowd of kids trying to beat the morning bell.

"You are sooo lucky," Becky grumbled when she caught up to Meg and Chris. "I asked my mom if I could drop out, too, and know what she said? 'No, we can't.' *We?* Do you believe it?"

"I wish you guys went to Crispin Landing Elementary instead of Roaring Brook," Meg said. "If it weren't for you, I probably would have dropped out after the first day. I brought you each a present." Meg reached into her backpack.

"Hey, neat," Chris said when Meg handed them each a paper bag marked *G.A.S.P. Survival Kit*. He tried on Meg's fake eyeball glasses. "Hey, they're horn rims, too. Very in-genius."

"You can look down at your desk and do your cartoons, and Mrs. Dunwoodie won't know the difference, ha, ha," Meg joked. "The markers and scissors are for some of your alien space vehicles."

"Thanks for this," Becky said, tying on the purple, green, and yellow friendship bracelet Meg had made for her.

"See, I started another one on the clipboard for you, so you can see the pattern," Meg said. "Next Tuesday, my mom and I are going shopping for new string at the Knit One shop. It's right across the street from the middle school, so if you don't have to go home right away, look around for us."

Becky scowled. "I only wish. But don't you remember? Next Tuesday after school, *we* have to go to the library to learn research skills. I just wish I could send my mom instead." Becky pulled out a balloon-trimmed box from her survival bag. "What's this?"

Meg lifted the lid to show her the stationery

inside. "When Chris is drawing his cartoons, you can send me notes about what's *really* going on in G.A.S.P. I think Erica and Suzi make up stuff to tell the kids at Crispin Landing Elementary on Tuesdays and Thursdays. Would you write to me and tell me what's really happening?"

Becky nodded and carefully put her survival kit into her backpack. She was going to have plenty of chances to use it.

When the three G.A.S.P.-ers got to Mrs. Dunwoodie's class, all the chairs were lined up in rows at the far end of the room.

"Wouldn't you know it?" Meg groaned. "We're going to have *Jeopardy* on my very last day."

Sure enough, Mrs. Dunwoodie's fake cardboard television screen was already propped up on the table with a huge stack of posterboard question cards next to it.

"Excuse me," Meg said, when she accidentally brushed Suzi Taylor's leg on her way to the back row of chairs.

Suzi flung back her bangs, looked at Meg, then turned to Erica. "Thank goodness it won't be so crowded in here after today."

Meg couldn't be sure, but she thought she heard Erica say something about Meg having to get back to her "little friends."

"One more reason you're lucky," Becky whispered when she squeezed in next to Meg. "You won't have to see those two Mondays, Wednesdays, and Fridays."

"I know, but it's just as bad hearing them brag like crazy on the two days they are at our regular school. They're always saying how easy the work is and how boring normal school is. They make G.A.S.P. sound like it's Disney World."

"Speaking of Disney World, here comes the White Rabbit," Chris said.

"We're late, we're late!" Mrs. Dunwoodie cried when she came in and checked the big clock on the wall. "Oh my. It's eight twenty-five already. On top of everything else, I'm afraid we won't have our usual thinking time this morning, class." Mrs. Dunwoodie rubbed the glass beads on her necklace together in a way that made Meg's hair stand on end. "The administration told me they need this room at nine this morning, and that we'll have to use a regular classroom until lunchtime!"

"Boo! Hiss!" a few kids called out, but no one really minded getting temporarily evicted as much as Mrs. Dunwoodie did.

"In any case, class, we must make the best of the situation, so today we'll start our *Jeopardy* match a bit earlier than usual."

Chris drew something on a piece of paper and handed it to Meg. "Pass it on." Inside was a frowning face he'd drawn with "Boo! Hiss!" inside a balloon.

Meg refolded it, and just as she was passing it on to Becky, Mrs. Dunwoodie spotted the note. "I'll have Margaret Milano up first and, I think, Suzanne Taylor. Suzi? Here on my right."

"Go, Meg," Becky whispered, patting Meg's arm. "Just think, you never have to do this again. Good luck."

For once, Meg didn't really mind about *Jeopardy* or getting up in front of the G.A.S.P.-ers. It was her last day, so what difference did it make how she did? On the other hand, Suzi Taylor was preening and smiling in front of everyone as if Mrs. Dunwoodie were filming the real *Jeopardy* for television. Or maybe a toothpaste commercial.

"Our category today is . . . Geography. Now, let's see what my mystery cards have in store for us this morning," Mrs. Dunwoodie said, shuffling the cards endlessly. Then, ever so slowly, she slid out one of them for the audience to view first.

"Oooo." "Hard." "Watch out up there." "A tough one," kids around the room murmured in fake horror.

Meg read the card. She couldn't believe it. Written in Mrs. Dunwoodie's giant printing was the word *Monrovia*. This was the same impossible geography fact that had knocked her out of the geography bee way before she ever began G.A.S.P.

"Suzi, would you begin?" Mrs. Dunwoodie asked.

When Suzi saw the card, she shrunk about two inches. "What is the capital of Nigeria?" she squeaked out in a not-so-Know-It-All voice.

"I'm sorry, Suzi," Mrs. Dunwoodie said sympathetically, as if a student had just died right there. "Meg?"

"What is the capital of Liberia?" Meg called out in a loud, clear voice.

"Very good, Meg," Mrs. Dunwoodie crooned. Meg couldn't help being pleased with the look of pleasant surprise on the teacher's face.

"Way to go, Meg!" she heard Becky's voice call all the way from the last row. Coming from the back row, too, were loud whistles and foot stomps. When Meg looked up to see who the noisemaker was, she saw Chris whistle again and adjust his fake eyeball glasses.

"Boy, you were amazing!" Becky said twenty minutes later when Meg finally returned to her seat clutching a fistful of ice-cream sandwich coupons. "Who woulda thunk a kiwi is a New Zealand bird? I thought it was some kind of furry fruit from California or someplace."

"If only these were tickets to Washington, D.C., like at the geography bee," Meg groaned, handing Chris and Becky some of the coupons.

"Oh, well, we've gotta celebrate your victory over the Don't-Know-It-Alls," Chris announced. "Even if it's just with free ice cream."

When the bell rang, Meg picked up her backpack. Even with six free coupons inside, it wasn't nearly as heavy as usual. Two more periods, lunch with Chris and Becky, then gym and Mock Trials, and her G.A.S.P. days would be over. The three friends went down the hall to the next class and for a change they took seats in the very first row.

"You know, Meg, this gym smells the same as my old Moylan School gym back in Hartford," Meg's dad said when the Milanos walked into the Crispin Landing Elementary School Science Fair. Mr. and Mrs. Milano liked nothing better than to talk about their old school days whenever they came to Meg's school. As they went on and on about all the nice teachers, mean teachers, and hard teachers they'd both had when they were little, Meg searched for her friends.

The gym was packed with kids, parents, and judges stooping over the exhibits and oohing and aahing over the amazing experiments. There were more dead plants killed by everything from soda to salt water than the day after a killer frost.

"There's Stevie, I think," Meg said to her parents when she spotted a familiar-looking head of scraggly hair over by the kindergarten exhibit. "See you in the auditorium for the announcements."

"Good luck!" Mr. and Mrs. Milano said, but Meg had already melted into the crowd.

Meg was curious about the exhibits lined up on long tables stretching the length of the gym, but she was more curious to see her friends. "I should have known I'd find you here," she said when she finally found everyone. "Right in front of a candy experiment."

"Boy, oh boy, why didn't we think of this?" Shana was saying to Stevie.

"Look what the kindergarten classes did, Meg. They counted to see if each bag of M&M's has the same number of colors. They don't. I knew it! I knew it!" Stevie cried as if she had personally discovered a new planet. "What a great idea!

Meg, do you have your clipboard? Write this down so I'll remember it. Next year, I'm going to count the number of pickles in every McDonald's hamburger I eat from now on."

Meg did have her clipboard, but she did not write down this information.

While Stevie and Shana studied the average number of M&M colors, Laura and Molly came over. "So, you survived G.A.S.P.," Laura said, linking her arm through Meg's while Molly did the same on the other side.

"How was it?" Molly said nervously. "Are you sorry?"

"Not a bit," Meg answered. "You won't believe this, but I won six of those dumb ice-cream sandwich coupons for being such a smarty-pants today. Even Mrs. Dunwoodie couldn't believe it! I almost offered the coupons to Erica and Suzi, but I couldn't do it. I wanted to, but I couldn't do it."

"You'd never be that mean." Laura looked proud that Meg hadn't acted like a Know-It-All even though she had been *the* Know-It-All on this particular day.

"You're sure you're not sorry?" Molly asked again.

"Don't worry, Molly, I'm really not. How can I be when I don't have one bit of homework this weekend? No Mock Trials to prepare. No Pencil Palaces to glue together. No geology models of Camden to design.''

''Why do I have the feeling I'm going to get a call at nine o'clock tomorrow morning with a new project you've cooked up for all of us?'' Laura asked Meg.

Meg smiled, and her smile grew bigger when she saw the judges in front of her project and Molly's. ''Look, there's Mr. Friedlander from Books 'N' Things looking at our projects, Molly. I didn't know he was a judge. I would have bought a few more Nancy Drews this week if I'd known he was judging the projects.''

''Well, our names aren't on them, just numbers,'' Molly said, though she looked as though she were about to tell Mr. Friedlander just who the brilliant scientist was who had put together one of the Camden models.

''Weshevyonetplzgtaorium,'' a voice boomed out of the loudspeakers up on the gym ceiling.

''What'd he say?'' Meg asked, looking around at everyone else's confused faces.

''We ask everyone to please go to the auditorium,'' the voice repeated, clearly this time.

''Oooo, it's time,'' Meg said, grabbing Molly's hand on one side and Laura's on the other. ''Let's find Shana and Stevie.''

"Just head for the food experiments," Laura said.

Sure enough, two aisles away, Stevie and Shana had to be dragged from a display about whether more people like chocolate chip cookies with or without nuts. On the way to the auditorium Meg had to explain to Stevie why this experiment was great for a first-grade class but just wouldn't do as a Friends 4-Ever project.

"Okay, okay," Stevie said when the lights dimmed, and Mr. Retzloff came onstage to welcome everyone to the judging.

"Once again, I'm happy to say that we did not blow up the science lab, although if anyone out there knows where our tarantula went, please see me after the awards are given out."

Grade by grade, Mr. Retzloff called out the names of the winners and made a few comments about the cleverness, creativity, or just plain practical thinking that went into each one.

"Nuts! The chocolate chip experiment didn't win," Stevie muttered after Mr. Retzloff handed a ribbon to a girl who had designed some planets out of Nerf balls in one of the lower grades.

"Now in our next grade, we have an unusual situation," Mr. Retzloff said. "We've never given out more than one blue ribbon before, but that's only because we never had two projects that coordinated in such a unique way."

"Unique, unique, it must be my Burglar Bag!" Stevie kidded.

Even in the dimly lit audience, Meg could see Erica and Suzi two rows ahead giving each other long, hopeful looks.

"Our judges have decided to award two blue ribbons. One will go to Molly Quindlen for her Camden watershed project and the other will go to Meg Milano for her Camden geology project."

"Yippee!" Molly cried, pulling Meg up from her seat. "We won, Meg! We both won!"

In a flash, Meg and Molly were up onstage shaking Mr. Retzloff's hand and trying not to drop the blue ribbons he handed each of them. "Great moments in science, you two," Mr. Retzloff said, beaming at his two students.

There was a roar of applause plus a few long whistles that came from the Friends 4-Ever row. Somehow, Meg managed to put one foot in front of the other so she could get back to her seat and the Crispin Landing Elementary School Science Fair could go on.

"You did it. You did it, you two!" Laura, Stevie, and Shana cried when the winning pair slid into their seats.

"We don't have any ice-cream sandwich coupons, but we wrote a note this afternoon and

made you guys presents in case you didn't win,"
Laura said. "Stevie, can you get it out of my tote
bag?"

"Not right now," Stevie answered. "In a few
minutes, after the awards are over."

"C'mon, Stevie. I want Molly and Meg to see
the note now," Laura said impatiently. "Never
mind, I'll get it out."

"I wouldn't do that," Stevie warned, but it
was too late.

"BRAAANG! BRAAANG!" An awful alarm
rang out when Laura reached down into her
ballet bag. About twenty heads in the immediate
rows swiveled around to check for smoke.

To quiet the awful sound, Laura tried to wrap
her jacket around the bag. "Would you discon-
nect this thing?" Laura hissed to the culprit.

Stevie reached for the bag and snapped a wire.
The terrible buzzing finally stopped. "I was just
trying to keep a burglar from stealing your ballet
slippers."

"Who would steal ballet slippers, Stevie?"
Meg cracked up. "The Sugar Plum Fairy?"

By this time, the audience was starting to
leave, no doubt relieved that they could go out
the regular doors and not the fire exits after all.

"Oh, Stevie," Laura sighed. "Just give Meg
the note, will you?"

Meg was still laughing while she unfolded Laura's unicorn stationery. Two all-blue friendship bracelets fell out, one for Molly and one for her. She began reading the note:

Dear Molly and Meg,
    Even if you don't win blue ribbons we wanted you to have these blue bracelets. Mr. Retz taught us a lot about science, but when we saw you make up and work together, you two taught us about how to be a friend.
                    Friends 'til the square dances,

        Laura and STEVIE

Who is the strange girl following Laura, and what does she want? Read Friends 4-Ever #8, MYSTERIOUSLY YOURS.